BOSS ALPHA

BOSS #5

VICTORIA QUINN

CONTENTS

1

HUNT

I UNDERSTOOD why Titan did what she did.

Didn't mean I was happy about it.

I didn't speak to her for four days. She didn't call me, and I didn't call her. We worked on our respective projects independently. Fortunately, we didn't have anything pressing to discuss for Stratosphere.

I focused on work and expanding my empire. When I was angry, I threw myself into work harder. I bought a whole food chain and invested in an online shopping retailer. I bought things left and right, looking for ways to expand my wealth as quickly as possible.

Money wouldn't make me happy. But it made me feel like I had control over something.

It was all I had right now.

I went out with Pine and Mike a few times. The

women were there, sliding their hands up my thighs and whispering dirty things into my ear. They wanted to be in my bed—even at the same time.

But I ignored their advances, only one woman on my mind.

My old lifestyle didn't interest me anymore. The second Titan walked into my life in those black stilettos, my world changed. The same old tricks didn't work anymore. The one-night stands were boring. My heart was no longer empty.

There was only one place I wanted to be, one bed I wanted to invade.

But I was too angry.

I wasn't ready to see her.

She didn't owe me anything. It wasn't like it was a secret. She told me this was her plan all along. I won her over, but with the snap of a finger, I lost her again. The universe didn't want us to be together.

Or someone didn't want us to be together.

On the fifth day, my knuckles finally relaxed and the rage dulled inside my chest. I could look at her without telling her she'd made a mistake. I could be calm and professional. I could be the man who preceded me by reputation.

I walked into Stratosphere with my paperwork tucked under my arm in a folder. I greeted our assistants then headed to her office. I knew she was there since the door was open. My knuckles tapped against the wooden door before I stepped inside.

She sat at her desk with a perfectly straight back. Her slender shoulders were elegantly poised, and her makeup highlighted the natural beauty of her features. She wasn't startled by my presence. She was a pro at hiding her emotions. Now that there was distinct distance between us, it was much easier for her to hide what she didn't want me to see. She wore a black jacket that was tight against her body, large black buttons reflecting the lights from up above. Diamonds gleamed from her earlobes, subtle but elegant.

I welcomed myself into her office and took a seat. I rested one ankle on the opposite knee, unbuttoned the front of my suit, and then laid the folder in my lap. Like nothing was different, I behaved as if this were any other meeting. She meant nothing to me. She was just a person sitting behind a desk.

She looked at me, her green eyes vibrant like a forest. She projected a hard exterior, but her smooth flesh suggested otherwise. I'd experienced all of her, and I knew there was nothing but softness under that tough exterior.

I noticed the engagement ring on her left hand, but I didn't allow myself to stare. I hadn't been expecting her to wear it, but it wouldn't make sense for her not to. Now

I would see her wear it all the time, publicly proclaiming her love for a different man.

We still hadn't spoken to each other, but that wasn't unusual for us. Our connection transcended words. "I've worked up a lot of ideas. I think we should coordinate with the stores and prepare for the holiday season. Experienced shoppers will hit the aisles before Thanksgiving even arrives."

After staring at me for a long minute, she nodded. "Lay them on me."

I placed a copy on her desk then went through my suggestions.

She listened to me, challenged me, and added her feedback. She was an easy partner because she was always honest with no ego. If I didn't like her idea, she brushed it off without conflict. Nothing was ever personal with her. She just wanted to do her job well.

After a few minutes of discussing back and forth, it started to feel normal again. We didn't talk about the engagement or how heavy that ring was on her finger. She didn't ask where I'd been the past week and I didn't ask what she did in her spare time.

We just stuck to business.

When we finished, I left the chair. "I'm heading back to my building. I'll see you later." I turned my back on her and walked out without waiting for a passionate goodbye. She wanted to remain professional at work, and that was easy for me to do. I thrived doing business, and since our personal relationship was so strained, this was much easier. I could stick to the facts. I could stick to the numbers.

I could stick to the bullshit.

A WEEK OF NOT GETTING LAID WAS TAKING ITS TOLL.

Titan came to me in my dreams, making me wake up warm and sweaty. My thoughts strayed when I was at work. I had a meeting with one of my executives, and while he droned on about quarterly profits, I imagined Titan sitting on my face.

I was hard up.

As much as I wanted her, I refused to cave. She had to come to me first. She had to tell me she wanted me. She had to remind me that she was still mine, inflate my hope like a balloon.

I sat on the couch in my living room, enjoying a glass of scotch while the game was on. I was in my sweatpants and shirtless, hoping Titan would pay me a visit at any moment. My phone was on the coffee table, but the screen was black.

I took a drink, letting the square ice cubes touch my lips as I drank. I'd told Titan to cut back on the alcohol, but I needed to take my own advice. I'd been drowning myself lately because it made me feel numb.

It was nice not to feel anything.

The elevator beeped, and the light above the doors lit up.

My eyes immediately shifted to the entrance, and my heart began to race. My cock hardened in my boxers, growing in expectation. Titan was on the other side. She was the only person who would drop by unannounced.

She was the only person with that right.

The doors opened, and sexy legs stepped inside, toned in the black heels. She was in the same gray dress as she wore earlier, the black jacket skintight and slimming.

I didn't rise from the couch. My elbows rested on my thighs, and I leaned forward. My head was turned her way, and I ignored the TV. The commentators rambled on in the background, so I grabbed the remote and turned it off.

She stood by the doorway and looked at me like she didn't know what to do next. There was only one reason for her visit, and she couldn't sugarcoat it.

She wanted me. Plain and simple.

She sauntered toward me, moving slowly as the tension escalated. Her eyes were locked on mine as her cheeks flushed with a wave of pinkness. Her fingers worked the front of her jacket, and she undid every button slowly.

My eyes never strayed from hers.

She dropped the jacket on the ground then moved into my lap. She pushed my shoulders against the couch and hiked up her skirt to her waistline.

She wasn't wearing panties.

Fuck.

She tugged the front of my sweatpants down until my length was revealed. She scooted up, grabbed me by the base, and then directed herself onto my length. She slowly lowered herself, her pussy slicker than it'd ever been since the day I met her.

She wanted me badly.

My hands moved to her hips, and I tugged her down until I was deep inside her. I could feel the tightness of her incredible pussy, the overwhelming wetness. She felt so good, like her pussy was made to fit my monster cock perfectly. "Miss me, baby?"'

Her hands snaked up my chest until she reached my shoulders. She dug her nails into my skin harshly, clawing at me so I couldn't get away. Her beautiful tits were hidden underneath her dress, but seeing her like this was just as sexy. Too anxious to feel me, she hadn't been able to wait to get everything off and onto the floor. "Yes."

I planted my bare feet on the floor, and I thrust into

her, sliding my soaked dick deep inside her. She moved with me, matching my pace perfectly. Her nails dug deep, and her breaths came out as pants. She breathed harder and deeper as she ground with me, dragging her clit against my pelvic bone. She didn't start off slow and gentle. She got right to the point, fucking my brains out because she was going crazy without me.

I'd been going crazy too.

We didn't share a single kiss because we used all our energy just to fuck. She slammed down on my dick, and I thrust hard into her, taking all of her pussy every single time. She knew how to take my enormous size like a real woman. She rode it deep and hard, knowing exactly how she liked to be fucked.

As did I.

Her fingers shook as they gripped my shoulders. She skipped breaths as she prepared to explode. Whimpers turned to moans, and soon she was screaming in my apartment, the sound joining all the faint echoes from our past.

I wanted to keep going, to make it a sex marathon like we used to have. But I hadn't gotten laid in too long, and she looked too damn sexy walking into my apartment without panties. She came here to fuck me. She couldn't handle the distance any longer. The silence killed her, the hormones suffocated her.

I released deep inside her, dumping more come than

I ever had. I filled every single inch of her, feeling my come dribble back out and toward the base of my length. I kept going, giving her more than she could hold.

She scratched her nails down my chest and moaned again, rolling her hips and enjoying the feeling of my explosion. She pressed her face to mine and slowly came down from the high, the tenderness stretching between us.

When we were both finished, we looked at each other with the same lust, like we hadn't been satisfied by that rendezvous. But there was depth in the look, feelings that were far more profound than sex.

I lifted her as I got to my feet, and I carried her into my bedroom. My cock was still inside her, where it would be buried for the rest of the evening. I hoped she'd been sleeping well, because neither one of us would get sleep tonight.

I set her on the bed and yanked her dress over her head. Her bra came next, and then she was finally naked underneath me, gorgeous and sexy. I gripped both of her tits because I missed them as much as I missed the rest of her. I got my sweatpants and boxers off then positioned myself on top of her, prepared to fuck her even harder than I just had. I was semihard, but I was quickly returning to full mast.

Her arms circled my neck, and she kissed me hard on

the mouth. "Give me all of your come, Hunt." She locked her ankles together against my back. "I missed it..."

———————

It seemed like we went back in time.

Now we were fucking the way we used to. We didn't talk about our lives. We didn't talk about anything. It was right to the point—and then she left. We really were just a hookup. I was a booty call.

I didn't ask her how she felt about being engaged to Thorn. I never asked if she was happy. I didn't want to know when they were getting married. I wasn't ready to listen to those painful words just yet.

I was still broken.

When I went to Stratosphere the next day, Titan was already in the conference room. We had a meeting with a few distributors for the East Coast, and coffee and snacks were supplied by our assistants. She sat at the end of the table, her tablet in front of her along with her notepad and pens. She wore a skintight red dress and black heels. Red was an intense color, and very few people could wear it so well. She made it look like a second skin.

I took a seat and opened my satchel.

She looked through her tablet, silently preparing for the meeting.

We didn't say hello.

It didn't seem like I fucked her for hours last night. There was no sleep in her eyes. She didn't appear to be tired at all even though she'd left my place around two in the morning. It shouldn't surprise me that we could sit together like this, as if last night hadn't happened.

But it still surprised me.

I caught the glimmer in the corner of my eye, the bright sparkle the reflected off the diamond on her hand. I didn't look directly at her ring because it would only piss me off. But it was distracting, the way it shimmered with the rainbow.

I finally turned my head and got a glimpse.

It was an enormous diamond in a white gold band. It was simple but enormous. Thorn cared more about making a statement with the jewelry he placed on her finger than giving her something she truly wanted.

Titan preferred subtlety.

If I bought her a ring, it would look much different from that.

I glanced away, hating myself for looking in the first place. "You want to lead this one?" I stared out the window because looking at the cityscape of Manhattan was far less painful than looking directly at her.

"Sure."

I'd led the presentation last time, so I didn't want to overstep by going first again.

She glanced at her watch. "They should be here any second. Anything we need to go over?"

I could crunch numbers and talk business all day. Titan made it easy. But we were so good together when we did other things. I hated this distance, this coldness. It was sickening. "No."

Titan lifted her gaze and stared at me. I wasn't looking directly at her so I wasn't sure if I was right, but I suspected I was. She stared at the side of my face, her green eyes burning into me like fire. I knew she wanted to say something, to address this tension between us. But picking at the seam would only force it to rip apart completely.

It was better to say nothing at all.

———————

I WALKED INTO THE RESTAURANT AND TOOK MY SEAT IN THE booth. We were at Charlie's Steakhouse, a popular place for lunch for executives. It was close to my office, along with everyone else's. It was hard to get a table, but I never had a problem getting in anywhere.

I sat across from Kyle Livingston, who had made it into town the night before.

I didn't waste any time getting an audience with him.

Kyle shook my hand. "How are things, Diesel?"

Fucking terrible. "Good enough. What about you?"

"My wife is pissed at me, but she's always pissed at me."

"What did you do this time?"

"Told her I didn't want to start a family just yet." He shrugged. "Work has been too hectic."

If Titan were my wife, I'd be knocking her up right now. "Work is work. Work shouldn't be life."

"Really?" He narrowed his eyes in annoyance. "You're the biggest workaholic I've ever met, and you're going to tell me that?"

I brushed off the comment by getting the waiter's attention and ordering a beer.

Kyle did the same. "So, how's your secret lover?"

I'd professed my love for a nameless woman the last time I saw him and Rick Perry. I'd been hoping to come clean about Titan's identity by now. Looked like that was going to be on hold for a while. "Good."

"Are you going to tell me who this woman is yet?"

"Nope." I took a drink before I commandeered the conversation. "I wanted to talk to about working with Titan. You both have the same interests, and you can both be vital to each other."

"Why are you talking about her when she's not here?"

It was a good question. Unfortunately, I didn't have a good answer. "Titan doesn't chase opportunities. She's too classy for that."

"Really?" he asked. "She seems like a hustler to me, but not in a bad way."

She was. She hunted her prey down until she got what she wanted.

"But, I just got a call from Vincent Hunt yesterday. He's the reason I'm in town..." His eyes drifted away along with his voice, understanding the obvious tension that filled the space around our table. Everyone in the industry knew my father and I weren't on speaking terms. They also knew about the little stunt I'd pulled. No one asked me about my father because they knew they wouldn't get an answer. And I knew no one was stupid enough to ask my father about me.

I shouldn't be surprised my father moved in on Kyle so quickly. When he didn't get his way with Titan, he was pissed. Now he had to make good on this threat and punish Titan for siding with me. It was a blow to his ego —because no one ever said no to him. "That's what I wanted to talk to you about."

"Your father?" he asked in surprise.

"Not him specifically, but what he's going to offer you."

"How do you know what he's going to offer me?" His beer had been set on the table minutes ago, but he hadn't had the opportunity to drink it. We'd been conversing too intently.

"Because he offered the same thing to Titan. She said no."

"What was the offer?" He didn't look at the waiter once the basket of bread was brought to the table. He didn't take his eyes off me as he ordered his lunch.

I ordered then handed the menus over. Once the waiter was gone, I continued. "He offered to get Titan into stores all over the world in exchange for five percent."

It took Kyle nearly a minute to process the deal. "And she said no because…?"

"She thinks the two of you could accomplish a lot more."

He cocked an eyebrow. "She thinks the two of us could do better than what Vincent Hunt offered? To get her products in everywhere with only five percent in return? I've been doing business a long time, and I've never heard a deal like that."

"Exactly." This deal had no effect on me whatsoever. I could have just let it go and moved on with my life. But my father was trying to screw with Titan, and I couldn't let that happen. Vincent played dirty, so I would play dirty too. "Titan thought it was too suspicious. Why would a man like Vincent Hunt make a deal like that? The second something doesn't make sense is when you should start worrying."

Kyle didn't seem totally convinced, but he didn't reject my thoughts altogether.

"I think his businesses are failing." That was a lie, and I felt a little guilty for spreading a false rumor about my father. It was wrong of me to tell the world about my relationship with my father—but at least the story was true. This was pure bullshit. "I think this is just a desperate move to ride Titan's coattails."

He crossed his arms over his chest, eyeing me closely.

"I think you should skip his offer. Don't even meet with him. Work something out with Titan. The two of you could be immensely beneficial to each other. You could both get what you want without having to give up a single part of your company. Sounds perfect to me."

Kyle rubbed his chin as his eyes shifted away from my face. He considered my words in silence, going over everything I said.

I hoped it was enough to entice Kyle. I couldn't let Titan lose this opportunity because of me. It was one of her biggest business goals. There wasn't a single doubt in my mind that she would find another way, but it would take her a long time.

Kyle finally spoke up. "It is suspicious..."

"Extremely."

"Titan is a smart woman. I trust her instincts."

Good.

"I already scheduled the meeting with Vincent, and I

don't want to cancel it so late. Wouldn't want to get on his bad side."

My father was a smooth talker. Hopefully, what I'd said today was enough to keep Kyle on our side. "How about I arrange a meeting with Titan for tomorrow afternoon?"

"I'll have my assistant take care of it," he said. "My schedule is pretty packed this week."

I wanted to push him a little harder, but if I made my aggression obvious, Kyle would become suspicious. "Sounds good." I soothed my nerves by taking a long drink of my beer. The frothy liquid went all the way down my throat, but it wasn't enough to calm my raging heart. I was the reason Titan had lost this opportunity.

I had to get it back.

2

TITAN

THERE WAS a distinct chasm between us.

Hunt was distant with me. There was an ice wall erected between us, an invisible line neither one of us crossed. He never mentioned my engagement to Thorn. He didn't try to convince me being with Thorn was a mistake.

He said nothing at all.

Now we worked together like two indifferent people.

I didn't like it.

But I knew that was how it had to be.

Thorn's ring felt heavy on my finger. It was a flawless diamond that still sparkled even when there was minimal light. It felt strange to wear it, like it didn't belong there. I received compliments on it everywhere I went, but as much as I smiled, those kind words didn't go to my heart.

All of it felt like a production.

A meaningless show.

A part of me thought it felt right, seeing the way Thorn smiled up at me. I felt safe with him, like there was no man in the world who would be better.

But I also couldn't stop thinking about Hunt.

And how much this hurt him.

The pain was obvious for both of us, and that's probably why we never spoke about it. Maybe we would never mention it. Maybe we would just hook up and say as little as possible. It was a sad thought to have, but I knew that would be the best outcome for both of us.

Because nothing would ever change.

I was sitting at my desk when Jessica spoke over the intercom. "I have Connor Suede on the line for you."

"Patch him through."

The light lit up on the receiver, and I hit the button before I took the call. "Hello, Connor."

"Titan." Mysterious as usual, he said more in silence than he did with words. "I love your voice. I see colors of black, gray, and red every time I hear it."

He was an artist, so it didn't surprise me when he said those sorts of things. They usually came off as sexy or romantic, whether he intended it that way or not. My fling with Connor had been nice because he knew how to please a woman, but also because he wasn't the commitment type of man. I hadn't seen him with a serious girlfriend since I met him years ago. And he never wanted anything serious with me. He respected the fact that I knew exactly what I wanted. "Thank you."

"Congratulations are in order."

"Thank you." I looked down at the ring on my finger, seeing the large diamond that was one of a kind.

"Thorn is a good man. I don't say that too often."

"I'm aware." Connor wasn't the best person to get right to the point. He kinda drifted around, working at his own pace. The only reason I didn't rush him was because I was a huge fan of his clothing line. I got early releases before they were even announced to the public. I loved his shoes, his clothes, and everything else he made. He was truly a genius at dressing a woman to make her look stunning.

"I'm calling because I sent one of my girls to your office. A gift from me to you."

I smiled. "I love your gifts."

"I was hoping you would wear it to the gallery tomorrow."

The function had completely slipped my mind. A coalition of some of the most amazing artists had come together to sell their pieces of art. I wasn't a big art collector, but if I saw something that spoke to my soul, I bought it. "Of course."

"I look forward to seeing you. Take care."

"Bye, Connor."

———

MY DRIVER TOOK ME BACK TO MY PENTHOUSE AFTER WORK. I sat in the back seat while we were stuck in rush-hour traffic. Everyone was going home or to the gym after a long day at the office. I took advantage of the time to call Thorn.

"Hey, what's up?"

"Did you forget about that gallery party we're going to tomorrow too?"

Thorn chuckled into the phone. "Now that you mention it, yes."

"Connor sent me a dress to wear. If he hadn't, I probably wouldn't go."

"Now you have to show it off."

"It's so gorgeous, I would wear it to bed."

He chuckled again. "That would be a waste. And you would need to iron it for hours to get all the wrinkles out."

"True. Do you have something to wear?"

"I'll throw on a suit. I've got hundreds of them."

"Alright. You want to pick me up?"

"Sure. I'll drive the new Ferrari I got."

"Ooh...sounds like fun."

"I love that you understand cars. All my girls like to ride in them, but they don't really love them the way you do."

"That would change if they were behind the wheel," I said. "That kind of power can go to anyone's head."

He had a smile in his voice. "What are you doing now?"

"I'm sitting in traffic on my way home. What about you?"

"About to head to the gym."

"Don't you ever get tired of going to the gym?" I never liked them. I'd rather starve than find the ambition to spend an hour on the treadmill.

"Yes. But I never get tired of getting laid."

I rolled my eyes.

"How are things with Hunt?" He dropped his playful attitude.

Once Hunt was mentioned, I turned serious too. "We haven't talked much."

He paused over the line. I imagined he was standing in his office, his gym bag sitting on the desk. "Does that mean you aren't seeing each other anymore?"

"We are...we just don't talk."

"I see."

"It's how it used to be when we first started seeing each other. Just sex and that's it."

"Is that a good thing?" he asked. "Sounds like exactly what you wanted."

"Yeah…I guess." I missed the connection we used to have, the openness. Now it was cold and empty. The silence was filled with all the conversations we never had. I'd made my decision that it would never work between us, but that didn't stop my heart from aching.

"You know I'm here to talk."

"I know, Thorn."

"I should get going, though. I'll talk to you tomorrow, alright?"

"Okay."

"And by the way, this new dress is short, right?" His playfulness picked up again.

"Actually, yes," I said with a grin.

"Perfect. My fiancée is going to be the hottest woman in the room tomorrow night."

"You're sweet."

"And you know what makes it better? You're the only woman I'm ever sweet to."

IT SEEMED LIKE HUNT WAS AVOIDING ME.

The last time we hooked up, I was the one who showed up on his doorstep.

He never came to me.

Since he was the one who usually couldn't keep his hands off me, it seemed strange. But I suspected his distance stemmed from his rage. He was pissed at me for saying yes to Thorn, even though I'd given him plenty of warning. Hunt hadn't let it go, and I wondered how long it would take him to accept the truth.

A part of me suspected he would stop seeing me. I didn't want to even think about it because that would be devastating. I'd grow crazy without having him between my legs. Seeing him with someone else in the tabloids would make me hurl. But if that were his decision, I'd have to accept it with a stoic expression.

Fortunately, the light brightened over the elevator and the doors opened.

Hunt stepped inside my penthouse.

He was in black jeans and a black t-shirt. Despite the dark color of his clothes, his skin still looked tanned. His hair was styled like he'd just gotten out of the shower not too long ago. I imagined he hit the gym after work before he headed over here.

I stood in the living room because I had just made myself a drink. I was still in my stilettos because I hadn't had a chance to slip them off yet. My bag was on the other couch, and I still wore the black jacket I'd put on in the car.

I froze in place when I looked at him, my fingers not sensing the cold glass in my hands. My heart stilled in my chest, but once the shock passed, it thumped harder than it did before. A tingling sensation erupted in my fingertips. The skin of my throat suddenly felt cold, desperate for his kiss. I wanted his hot breaths to warm me up, to fall across my skin and make me writhe. I wanted to be loved by this man, suffocated by his powerful affection.

He walked across the room toward me, and even though he moved at a normal pace, it seemed to take forever. He wasn't moving quickly enough. His hands weren't on me fast enough. His eyes burned into mine with their usual look of possessiveness. He undressed me with just a look, stripping off my dress and then my bra and panties. His eyes made love to my entire body even though he still hadn't touched me.

He crossed the room and stopped right in front of me, peering down at me with an aggressive presence.

I forgot to breathe.

He wrapped his hand around my glass, and he placed it on the coffee table without taking his gaze away from mine. His neck didn't have to crane so drastically to look at me because my heels made me five inches taller. But even in the stilettos, I felt tiny in comparison to his height and build.

With his eyes locked to mine, he grabbed my left hand. His fingers found my diamond ring, and he pulled it off my finger. I didn't wear it around the house, but I hadn't had a chance to take it off. He dropped it on the sofa table then finally stepped farther into me. His hard chest pressed against my soft tits through my clothing. His mouth scooped up mine in a heated kiss, all lips and no tongue.

That kiss...

His hand moved underneath the fall of my hair until he got most of it in his fist. He gave a slight tug, like I was a horse on a rein. He pivoted my mouth exactly where he wanted it to be and enjoyed me, kissing me precisely the way he wanted to.

His other hand gripped the back of my dress, making it rise up my body as he bunched up the fabric. More kisses ensued. Our mouths combined, burned, and then they broke apart again so we could breathe. When we came together again, it felt better than the last time we touched. He was making my wet, making me soak my panties with desire. His hand squeezed my dress again before it slid up, and he grabbed the zipper at the top. He slowly dragged it down, opening the back of the dress until he stopped just above my ass. The dress came loose over my shoulders and started to sink to the floor.

He pushed it down, revealing me in my black bra and thong. He tugged on my hair again and kissed me harder. "Damn." He pulled me into his hard chest and moved his tongue in my mouth, making it dance with mine erotically. Our touches escalated, our breathing heightened. I felt my pussy tighten even though it didn't have a cock to grip. I wasn't thinking about my engagement to Thorn, Illuminance, or anything else. I was just thinking about the man who was enjoying me so profoundly.

His hand casually popped my bra open so it could fall to the floor. He pulled the straps off my shoulders and slid it off my body. When I was in just my black thong, he broke our kiss so he could look at me. Possessive, territorial, and aggressive, he stared down at me like I was his forever. He palmed one tit with his large hand and gave it a firm squeeze while his hand remained in my hair. His eyes roamed down the valley between my breasts, over my flat stomach, and to the lacy panties that were about to be stripped away. "On your knees." He issued the command like a general, leaving no room for misinterpretation.

He was in charge tonight.

I wanted to be the one calling the shots, but tonight, my body didn't seem to mind. It came to life at his command, making me feel submissive. I wanted to be ordered around. I wanted to obey. I wanted to be whatever he wanted me to be.

So I sank to the ground. My knees hit the rug, which was little respite from the hardwood floor. My legs folded, and my ass sat on the back of my heels. My stilettos were still on, and they slightly dug into my skin. I tilted my head up to look at him.

He stared down at me with a look of aggressive violence. He enjoyed the view long before he did anything about it. His chest puffed out with a deep breath, he clenched his jaw, and then he undid his jeans. The zipper came undone, and soon his pants were around his ankles. His boxers came next, revealing his enormous cock that was already oozing at the tip. His hand moved into my hair, and he grabbed himself by the base. He pointed his dick at my mouth and pushed inside before my lips had even begun to part. "Open wide."

I opened my mouth as wide as I could and flattened my tongue.

He didn't hesitate before he plowed deep down my throat, fucking my mouth vigorously. Saliva pooled at the corners then dripped down my chin. My eyes burned with unemotional tears and streaked down my cheeks. The sensual and soft kiss we had just shared was replaced by a deep-throat fuck.

But it felt good.

He gripped the back of my neck and pushed harder. His big dick wasn't gentle against my tongue and mouth. He hit me deep and hard, plowing me ruthlessly like I hadn't sucked him off in years.

His face was etched in fine lines of pleasure. He

breathed hard as he enjoyed my wet mouth. The saliva dripped down his base and to his balls. From there, it leaked to the rug beneath us. "Fuck." He pulled himself out of my mouth suddenly, edging himself so he wouldn't release in my throat.

He got to his knees on the rug and positioned himself behind me. His hand dug into my hair, and he pressed my face against the rug, making my ass pop up in the air. He widened his stance then shoved himself inside me.

I moaned at his size. I'd had him so many times, but I was never prepared for how amazing it felt. He was all man, thick like a tree trunk and long like a pipe. His hand gripped me by the back of the neck, and he kept my face to the ground as he fucked me right in the middle of the living room floor.

I'd never been fucked quite like this.

His other hand held on to my hips, pulling himself into me with every thrust. He commandeered the night, taking me roughly just the way he wanted. A moan emerged from him between his thrusts, enjoying every second of my immense tightness. I had the perfect pussy for his big dick, and he enjoyed every second of it.

He scooped his arm around my chest and yanked me upward, giving his dick to me at a different angle. He pressed his mouth just behind my ear and thrust into me, his other hand wrapped around my stomach. He hit harder and harder, fucking me like he'd never had me before.

My hands reached behind my back, and I gripped his hips, using him as an anchor to pull myself back into him. I wanted more of that cock than he could possibly give. Another inch and he would hit my cervix and make me cringe in pain. My ass smacked against his body over and over as we fucked on the ground like a pair of wild animals.

My hands gripped his wrists as I was pushed into a powerful orgasm. My moans turned into screams that filled my penthouse. It felt so good, so deep. My screams became incoherent, and my head felt lopsided from the high I had just achieved.

He held on to my hips and made his final thrusts before he came deep inside me, making sure I got every drop of his precious come. He groaned in my ear, not suppressing his obvious pleasure.

I loved feeling full of him like this. I loved his weight, his warmth. It made me feel like the most desirable woman on the planet when I was pumped full of his arousal. When he released me, I moved my hands to the floor as I held myself up on all fours.

He slowly pulled out of me and disappeared into my bathroom.

I took a minute to gather myself, to remember the exact spot where we fucked. I hadn't done it on the floor like that for as long as I could remember. I may never have done it that way. It was carnal and aggressive, ruthless and borderline barbaric.

Hunt returned a moment later after he was cleaned off.

I sat up then slipped off my heels before I rose to my feet.

Hunt pulled on all his clothes, ran his fingers through his hair, and then kissed me on the cheek.

He'd never kissed me on the cheek before.

"Goodnight." He walked to the elevator.

What?

"Are you leaving?"

He hit the button then turned around. "Yes."

I didn't know what to make of it because he never dropped by, fucked me, and then left immediately afterward. We spent time in bed, made love a few more times, and then he departed long after midnight. Now he was trying to get in and out quicker than going through a fast-food drive-thru. "Why?"

He narrowed his eyes at me harshly, like I'd said the wrong thing. "You know why." The doors opened so he stepped inside.

I walked to the elevator buck naked and hit the button so the doors would remain open. "Get your ass in here."

He didn't move.

"Now."

He sighed before he stepped back inside my penthouse. The doors immediately closed behind him. He crossed his arms over his chest and stared at the penthouse like it was the first time he'd walked inside. His jaw clenched with hostility. He was obviously angry at me. Livid, to be more correct. "I'm not handling this well. I thought I would be over it by now, but I guess I'm not."

I knew all this derived from my engagement to Thorn. We still hadn't talked about it, and it was obviously heavy on his mind.

He slid one hand into the front pocket of his jeans then ran his other hand through his hair.

I didn't know what to say to improve the situation. I hated hurting him. I didn't do it on purpose. Hurting him was the same thing as hurting myself. I wanted to apologize for it, but that was inappropriate. I had nothing to be sorry for. There was no other decision I could have made.

"I know you don't love him." His eyes were on the kitchen even though he wasn't really looking at it. "Not the way you love me. I know he's just a friend you've chosen as family. I even like the guy. But...it hurts."

My eyes contracted as the pain swept through me.

"It hurts for a lot of reasons. But the biggest reason of all...it should be me."

I didn't want to hear this. I didn't want to go in a

circle again. "Hunt, we can't keep talking about this...it's not going to make either one of us feel better."

He shook his head slightly before he looked at me again. He stared at me for a long time, seeing something that only he could see. He watched me closely, his brown eyes soaking in every aspect of my expression. He stared for so long that minutes seemed to pass. "You're right. It's not." He hit the button to the elevator again.

My heart fell back into my stomach as I watched him step inside. "Hunt..."

"What?" He held the door open, watching me with a slightly irritated expression.

Now I was the one to stare at him. I stared at the scruff along his jaw and fell into the darkness of his eyes. It was time for me to say something, but not a single word formed on the tip of my tongue.

"What?" he repeated, his voice sounding deeper. "If you want me to stay, say it."

I didn't want to watch those doors close and hide his face. The night I said I was going to say yes to Thorn's proposal, the doors had shut on Hunt's expression. My stomach filled with acid, pain, and tears. I couldn't wipe the image from my memory. "Please."

"Please what?" he pressed.

"Stay."

Our eyes remained locked for several heartbeats before he stepped back inside my penthouse. His hostility disappeared at my plea, and he slid his hands into my hair before he kissed me. As if the living room floor hadn't happened, he kissed me as if he hadn't already had me tonight.

He kissed me like he'd never had me.

His powerful arms circled me before they lifted me into his chest. Without breaking his stride, he carried me out of the living room and into my bedroom. He placed me on the bed and smothered me with hot kisses. His lips reached the hollow of my throat and made me writhe on the bed. Like he hadn't just made me come, I needed him to make me come again.

His jeans came undone, and he pushed his bottoms down again. He pulled my hips to the edge of the bed, and he shoved his throbbing cock inside me once more, burrowing deep between my legs, right where it belonged. He moaned from the back of his throat as he enjoyed my usual wetness.

I grabbed on to his hips and slowly tugged him inside me, wanting that soft rocking he usually gave me.

He thrust at a perfect pace, his hands holding him over me on the bed. His powerful body flexed and moved as he rocked into me, making love to me at a sensual pace. His eyes darkened as he looked at me, claiming me all over again. He was angry, but he was also deeply affectionate like he'd always been. "Baby..."

My hands ran up his chest as I was swept away by

our passion. "Diesel..."

THE VALET TOOK THORN'S CAR KEYS BEFORE THORN TOOK my hand and we walked inside. Reporters were on the sidewalk, and they snapped a few pictures of us before we stepped inside the building.

The large lobby was decorated for the occasion with gold streamers and black tables. Paintings hung on the walls, and waiters passed with a tray of champagne. New York's finest mingled together in their expensive gowns and suits.

Thorn kept his grip on my hand as he pulled me inside. "Champagne okay?"

"Sure."

He grabbed me a glass then placed his hand on the small of my back. His affection felt natural because we'd been doing it in public for over a year. I was used to Thorn touching me, and it never made me uncomfortable. When his hand was on me, I actually felt more relaxed. He was my best friend as well as my family.

We mingled with a few people, all of whom complimented my dress as well as my ring.

"So, when's the big day?" Claudia Sawyer, the editor for the biggest fashion magazine in the world, asked.

Thorn and I hadn't even discussed it.

"Not sure yet," I answered. "We're just enjoying being engaged."

His arm moved around my waist, and he pulled me closer to his side. "I'm kinda in a rush for the bachelor party, so I'm sure we'll decide something quickly." He winked at me.

I chuckled at his wickedness. "Your bachelor party will be nothing compared to mine."

"Ooh..." Claudia laughed. "Looks like you met your match, Thorn."

Thorn eyed me fondly. "I think I did."

We spoke with a few other people Thorn knew from his social circles. I saw a couple people I wanted to see, but we were doing so much talking, I never really had a chance to look at any of the paintings.

Thorn was in the midst of a detailed conversation about sports, so I broke away to take a look at some of the artwork on the walls. One in particular was full of splashes of color. It was loud, vibrant, and it was nearly screaming even though it didn't make a sound. I stared at it for a few heartbeats before I moved on to the next piece, something more subdued. It fit my personality much better, and I took a moment to enjoy it.

"What do you think of this one?" A brunette in a silver dress stepped in front of a painting down at the end of the wall. She wore black heels with a black clutch in her hand. She was pretty and cheerful.

A man in a black suit joined her and stared at the painting, silent and brooding. He had muscular shoulders and a slim waistline.

He captured my notice out of the corner of my eye because he reminded me of Hunt. When I snuck a peek and turned my head completely, I realized it was him. I quickly turned away and pretended not to be staring.

But my heart plummeted out of my chest.

"It doesn't mean anything to me," he said quietly. "I've never been a fan of art."

"How can you not be a fan?" She stepped to the next painting. "It is beautiful."

"I guess we have different definitions of beautiful." He followed her and examined the next painting in line. His hands rested in his pockets, but his posture remained perfectly upright, rigid and strong.

I wanted to walk away and pretend I hadn't seen him, but if I moved too quickly, he would notice me. A wave of jealousy ran through me that I could barely control. I had no right to be jealous just because he was talking to some woman. I shouldn't jump to conclusions. But I didn't like what I saw.

They moved farther down the line, and she stopped in front of the painting. "You have to like this one, Mr. Hunt."

Mr. Hunt.

Hunt stared without any discernible reaction. "Can't say I do."

"But it's beautiful," she said. "Look at all the bright colors."

He shrugged and turned toward me, about to reach my side. "I guess I don't like bright colors." His eyes focused on me like he knew I'd been there the entire time. "Now this one..." He came to my side, his shoulder almost touching mine. "This one, I like. What do you think?"

I knew he was talking to me. "I like it too."

The brunette joined him and stared at the picture. "Yeah, it's pretty good." She crossed her arms over her chest.

Hunt stood far closer to me than he did to her. "Olivia, let me introduce you to my business partner, Titan."

Olivia smiled before she shook my hand. "A pleasure. I've spoken to your assistant a few times."

I smiled as I shook her hand, still having no idea who she was. "Nice to meet you as well."

Hunt grinned as he watched me uneasily, probably picking up the waves of jealousy I felt. "Olivia is one of my assistants and has fine taste in art. She was giving me some pointers."

Humiliation washed over me at the way I'd overreacted. I hadn't said or done anything, but Hunt knew I'd

had a silent freak-out behind the mask I wore. I was terrified he'd brought a date to the art gallery and I'd have to
watch some woman drool all over him. "That's nice of
her to help you even when she's off the clock. She must
like you...although I can't imagine why."

He smiled at my playful jab.

"Mr. Hunt is wonderful," Olivia said. "When I had
my first baby, he gave me nine months of maternity leave
—with pay."

Now I noticed the wedding ring on her left hand.
That was something I would have picked up on if I
hadn't been so flustered. "He sounds like a good boss."

"He's the best." Olivia patted him on the shoulder
before she stepped away. "I need to track my husband
down. I'll see you later, Mr. Hunt."

Hunt turned his gaze back to the painting. "Have a
good night, Olivia."

She disappeared, leaving us alone in front of the
painting.

Hunt hadn't dropped his smile.

So infuriating. "What?"

He turned to me, the gleam in his eyes. "I was on the
other side of the room, and I could still tell you were
jealous."

"I wasn't jealous," I lied. "I just wasn't sure if it
was you."

"Bullshit. You know it's me before you even get a look

at me."

I usually could feel him before my eyes actually caught a glimpse. His intensity was sound waves, and my body was the radar. I could detect his heat, his energy.

"You're here with your fiancé, but you're losing your mind over me and some woman." He turned back to the painting. "I find that interesting."

I rolled my eyes. "You're worse than I am."

"True. But at least I admit it." He pivoted his body toward me and moved his hand to my hip.

I immediately stopped breathing, my heart stopping at the same time.

He was far too close to me than he should be. He could kiss me if he wanted. He could take my breath away if he wanted. His dark eyes homed in on my lips, and he leaned in.

But I didn't pull away.

He pressed his mouth to my cheek and kissed me.

It was innocent and soft, but it made my legs quiver. It made my knees want to fall apart so his lips could kiss my most sensitive features. The kiss was merely polite for a social event, but I couldn't stop picturing him fucking me in my bed. I couldn't stop thinking about the way he came inside me three times last night. I'd had so much come in my pussy that it wouldn't fit. My skin flushed with searing heat, and an almost silent moan escaped my throat.

But I bet Hunt could hear it.

He pulled away and dropped his hand.

I opened my eyes and looked at the intensity in his gaze. He was staring at me the way he did when we were alone together. Everyone else in the room saw me in the beautiful dress Connor gave to me, but Hunt saw something completely different.

I was buck naked.

I was covered in sweat.

I was in his bed.

Stuffed with his come.

His hands rested in the pockets of his slacks, but his eyes violated me in ways that no one understood. Everyone carried on with their conversations and enjoyed their glasses of champagne, but Hunt and I made love with just our gazes. He licked his tongue up my neck to the hollow of my throat. He kissed me in all the places I desired. He worshiped me like the only woman he wanted in his sheets.

It seemed to go on forever.

We were interrupted by Connor Suede. If he hadn't come by, it probably would have continued on indefinitely. "Sweetheart, you look stunning." His arm circled my waist, and he kissed me on the cheek.

I almost pushed him off because Hunt was standing there. I knew he hated Connor and was fiercely jealous of him. Even though there was nothing between us now,

Connor was a handsome man I'd taken to bed before. I wouldn't want to even look at a woman Hunt had been with. "Thank you, Connor. How's your evening?" I quickly moved away from his embrace without appearing rude. I wouldn't put it past Hunt to punch anyone in the face for touching my hand a little too long.

"It's great." He wore all black, black jeans, t-shirt, and a leather jacket on top. "I just bought a painting to add to my collection."

"That's wonderful. It doesn't surprise me that an artist appreciates art."

Connor turned to Hunt and extended his hand. "Hunt. Good to see you."

Hunt shook his hand but only nodded in return.

Connor brushed off his coldness or didn't seem to notice. "I was wondering if you would do another photo-shoot with me next week."

"Again?" I asked in surprise.

"Sales are through the roof. You've branded my clothes in a way I never anticipated. Your image and your bravery are something woman desire. When that story hit the newspapers, it helped my sales—not made them worse. Women all over the world admire you. Something terrible happened to you, but you didn't give up." He held up his finger. "That's the kind of role model young women should be looking up to."

His words left me speechless because Connor was

never kind without reason. If he gave a compliment, it was genuine. If he didn't like you, he had no problem announcing it. He cared very little about what other people thought. Instead, he valued his own opinion above the rest. "That's sweet, Connor."

"So let's do another. I'm releasing a new evening fashion line." He indicated my dress. "From what I hear, people already love it."

"It is beautiful." I ran my hands down the front.

"Is that a yes?" he asked.

"Of course."

"That's wonderful." He leaned in to kiss me on the cheek again.

This time, Hunt didn't let the second kiss slide. He discreetly maneuvered between us and addressed Connor directly. "I've been meaning to get a new suit. Do you have any recommendations?"

Connor didn't pick up on the hostility because Hunt hid it well enough. "I have tons, actually."

"We should discuss it," Hunt said. "Titan is my business partner, and she speaks highly of your work. Perhaps I should adopt some of her taste in fashion."

"You can always swing by the office and one of my girls will fit you."

"Sounds like a great idea."

Connor was called away by someone, so he left abruptly.

The second he was gone, Hunt wore his fierce scowl. He eyed Connor's back like his gaze was a sharp knife and Connor was a cutting board. Hunt watched him closely before he turned back to me.

I couldn't suppress my grin. "And I'm the jealous one..."

He didn't crack a smile. "He wants to fuck you."

"So what?"

The hostile glare he gave me was hot enough to burn lava. "*So what?*"

"Just because he wants to doesn't mean he gets to. There are lots of women who want to hop into your bed. Does that mean you're going to screw all of them?"

His terrifying gaze was the only response I was going to get. "I don't want him to kiss you like that."

"He's French."

"Don't give a damn what he is."

"You're overreacting."

"Watch a woman kiss me on the cheek twice and see if I'm overreacting." He stepped away from me and returned to the main party, his powerful shoulders tense with unpleasant hostility. He entered the crowd but stuck out like an island in the middle of the sea. Even from across the room, I could feel his anger.

I could feel his rage.

3

HUNT

I SHOULDN'T HAVE LOST my temper over Connor.

Right now, it didn't matter. My only chance at keeping Titan was by making her fall so deeply in love with me that she would take one last risk for me. She would go against the evidence and choose to believe me just because she wanted to.

Acting like a jealous maniac wasn't the way to accomplish that.

Nor was storming out of her penthouse after fucking her.

I needed to get my shit together.

Connor was the last thing I should be worried about right now.

I had more pressing problems at the moment.

Natalie's voice interrupted my thoughts as I sat at my desk. "Sir, I have Kyle Livingston on line one."

I knew exactly what this was about, and I hoped it would be good news. My father could turn anything into gold with the snap of a finger. People found his intimidation respectable, so everyone wanted to do business with him. He was cunning but also eloquent. If we weren't at war with each other, I would actually admit I respected him as a businessman. He made great choices, and to the best of my knowledge, he'd never maliciously screwed anyone over. His business operated with some sense of morality. "Thank you, Natalie." I hit the speakerphone button so I could continue looking out the window. "What can I do for you, Kyle?" Playing it cool was the only way to operate. Men didn't respond to the pathetic sound of desperation. I was absolutely desperate at the moment, but I was far too proud to reveal it.

"Talked to your father yesterday."

"Is that so?" I kept up the pretense of indifference. My desires couldn't be obvious to anyone. If people understood your motives, they could easily turn you into a puppet. "How'd that go?"

"He offered the exact deal you predicted."

"And that's surprising?" I rested my elbow on the desk and propped my head against it. It was a sunny day in the city, not a cloud in the sky. But the presence of winter was obvious when people walked down the street in their thickest clothes.

"Guess not."

I got right to the point so I could act natural. It was something I would ordinarily do if I had no personal interest in the manner. "Are you going to take the deal?"

"I told him I would think about it."

It was an awfully great offer to turn down. The fact that Kyle had doubts boded extremely well for me.

"I thought the entire thing was suspicious. Why would he offer me something like that unless there's a catch?'"

"There's always a catch. And some things are too good to be true."

"That's what I was thinking."

"Well, let me know what you decide. Titan is still interested, but if you do decide to work with Vincent, she'll start working on a new plan." Lighting a fire under Kyle's ass would help. Titan wasn't the kind of woman to sit around and wait for things to happen. She *happened* to things. There was a solution to every problem, and she would always find it. "We have a meeting with some of my distributors next week, so we'll start from there." I held a terrible hand of cards, and I was bluffing. There was no meeting. There were no distributors. I needed Kyle, but I wasn't going to say it. Men with little power always let their egos inflate the second they had a bit of control. Men with a lot of power never let it go to their head because they were used to holding all the cards.

"Actually, I think working with Titan would be the better option for me."

A grin immediately spread across my face. I straightened in my chair and felt my chest relax for the first time that week. I'd finally gotten something done. I got Titan what she deserved, and I'd thwarted my father's spiteful plan. "I agree. I'll talk to Titan, and her office will contact you."

"I'd like to do this sooner rather than later before I formally turn down Vincent's offer."

"I understand." If it didn't work out with Titan, he didn't want to lose the only other deal he had on the table. "You'll hear from her in the next hour." I hung up then vacated my chair. I had a meeting in thirty minutes, but that didn't seem important right now. I stepped out and walked up to Natalie's desk. "Reschedule my meeting."

Natalie hid her surprise at the short notice. Instead, she nodded. "Of course, Mr. Hunt."

I never rearranged my life for anyone. In my world, everything revolved around me. I never dropped a business meeting for a woman or anyone else. But for Titan, nothing else seemed as important as she did.

TITAN WAS ON THE PHONE IN HER OFFICE AT Stratosphere. She looked up at me as I walked inside but still carried on her conversation like she didn't have company. "Yes, I think that's an excellent idea, Roger. We'll discuss it over lunch next week." She listened to him say something in return before she responded. "Sounds good. Take care." With candy-apple colored fingernails, she set the phone on the base then turned her full attention on me. She did a much better job of seeming indifferent toward me when we were in public, but she couldn't hide it completely. Her eyes held a different kind of intensity that was only reserved for me. She swallowed a lot more often and squeezed her legs together when she sat in a chair. Her eyes smoothed over my body like she was imagining her hands pressing against my solid chest. "I wasn't expecting to see you for at least another hour."

I shut her office door before I came closer to her desk. "Me either."

She glanced at the door before she turned back to me again, her guard up. She probably assumed I wanted to do something dirty right up against the window. That wasn't my intention, but her assumption wasn't unfounded.

I stood with my hands in my pockets as I stared down at her, looking at the hollow of her throat. It seemed so lonely in the blouse she wore. It needed to be warmed by my kisses, caressed by my callused fingers. When I looked at Titan, I didn't just see a beautiful woman—I saw my woman.

When she spoke, her voice was much quieter than usual. She was vulnerable when it was just the two of us, treating me like her lover even when she didn't want to. It was a natural urge, and I did the exact same thing. "What is it, Hunt?"

"I just talked to Kyle Livingston."

Her eyes narrowed at the mention of his name.

"He wants to do business with you. He's waiting for a call from your office." It gave me a great sense of pride that I could return this to her. I was like a dog that hunted down a squirrel in the backyard. Now I was bringing it to my master so I could be showered with praise. Her opinion meant the world to me.

"With me?" she asked in surprise. "What about Vincent?"

"Kyle turned down his offer. He wants to work with you instead."

Her eyes remained fixed as she slowly cocked her head to the side. She regarded me with intense suspicion, as if I'd just spoken in a different language to her. "Why would he want to do that?"

I shrugged. "Doesn't matter. Call him."

She pressed her hands against the desk and slowly rose to her feet. In heels, she was nearly eye level with me. I liked it when she had an extra five inches on her height because it was easier to kiss her, but I also liked it when she had to completely crane her neck just to meet my gaze. "It does matter. Kyle Livingston would have to be an idiot to reject that offer. Unless he's in love with you like I am, it doesn't make any sense."

I loved hearing her say that. I never got tired of it. She said it simply, like it was the truest thing in the world. It was innate and unstoppable. She had no shame admitting her feelings for me because they were an essential part of who she was. "He's not in love with me, so you don't need to be jealous."

When she glared at me, it was with distinct playfulness.

"I talked him into it."

"How on earth did you do that?" she asked incredulously.

"I told him you were the better partner. Simple as that." I held her gaze, wishing I could run my hand through her soft curls. I wished this enormous desk weren't between us so my hands could slide around her waist and pivot her against me.

She stared back at me like similar thoughts were going through her mind. Her playful glare and skepticism quickly slipped away, replaced by a touched expression. She grew softer as she faced me, becoming more vulnerable with every passing second. "Diesel..."

I moved around the desk and came to her side, my hands aching to touch her.

"I can't believe you did that."

Our rule of professionalism went out the window, and I grabbed her by the hips and turned her toward me. My hands ran across her ass then up her back as my body moved deeper into hers. I didn't kiss her, but the spark between us was smoldering enough. I looked into her face and saw so much of my own love reflected back at me. "Is it really that surprising?" My hand cupped her cheek, and my thumb brushed against her bottom lip. Her face was small in comparison to my enormous palm.

"No..."

"I'm not gonna let you get hit in the cross fire between my father and me. He can do whatever he wants to me, but he'd better leave you out of it."

"When he finds out, he's going to be mad."

My father was a prideful man. Of course this would tick him off. I'd managed to steer both Titan and Livingston away from him. He wouldn't take it lying down. He would be even less merciful in his next attack. But as long as his rage was directed toward me and not my woman, I didn't care. "I hope he is mad." I couldn't deny my urges anymore, and I leaned in and kissed her softly on the lips.

She kissed me back, her hands immediately moving to my chest. Her fingertips pressed through my clothing and applied pressure directly to my skin. She breathed into my mouth with a quiet moan, and I knew if she were sitting, she'd be squeezing her thighs together tightly.

My hand squeezed her ass then slowly pulled her skirt to her waist. My fingertips slid across her smooth skin, feeling the beautiful flesh I loved to enjoy every single night. My cock was hard against the zipper in my slacks, and he wanted to break free and dive between the legs of the most beautiful woman on the planet.

She kissed me harder and allowed her bare ass to be revealed in the middle of her office. But then she came to her senses and pulled her delicious lips away from mine. "We can't..." She stepped back and yanked her skirt down, flustered and aroused at the same time.

My fingers ached in pain, and my jaw was clenched with annoyance. I wanted to make love to her on that desk, to have her legs spread wide for me while she lay back on the wood. I wanted to take Tatum Titan in her natural habitat. But I shouldn't be surprised that her need for professionalism outweighed her desire. Her ambition was the only thing strong enough to combat it. Despite my raging hard-on, I respected her restraint. "Then I expect you to show me your gratitude later tonight."

She smoothed out the front of her skirt then touched her lips like I'd just bit her. "Show my gratitude, huh?"

My eyes moved to her lips, imagining them sucking my cock and devouring my come. "Yes."

"It's been a while since I've been in charge..."

"Too bad." My hand fisted into her hair, and I gave her an abrupt kiss on the lips before I walked away. "Let me know how it goes with Kyle. I told him the two of you could do great things together."

"I will." Her eyes followed me as I walked out.

I opened the door and turned around to look at her. "You'll get my instructions in a few hours."

She crossed her arms over her chest, wearing a defiant expression. But she didn't voice her disobedience.

I didn't expect anything in return for helping her. My only motive was to give her what she deserved. But if I could take advantage of the situation, I sure as hell would. "Have a good day, Titan."

"You too, Hunt."

WHEN I FINISHED MY SESSION AT THE GYM, I GOT INTO THE back seat of my Mercedes, and my driver escorted me back to my penthouse. My mind had been stuck on sex all day, and now that working hours were officially over, I called Titan.

She answered professionally, telling me she wasn't at liberty to speak her mind. "Titan."

I loved the way she said her own name. It was with so much confidence. "I have instructions for you."

"I'm listening."

"Go home. Get naked. Grab a bottle of lube. Finger yourself until you're ready for me."

"I don't need to do that to be ready for you, Hunt."

She had the wrong location in mind. "Actually, you do. And I strongly recommend it."

Her silence was the confirmation I was looking for.

"On all fours on the bed." I hung up and shoved the phone into my pocket. My eyes stared out the window, but I didn't see the buildings and the pedestrians. All I saw was Titan with her ass in the air, her fingers buried inside her asshole as she prepared to take my enormous dick. I didn't want to say a single word to her. I just wanted to fuck her, to remind her she was mine even if she wore another man's ring.

I went home, showered, and then changed into jeans and a t-shirt before having my driver drop me off at her building. I walked into the lobby, found the elevator, and slowly rose to the top of the building.

My heart was beating so fast.

I got off on calling the shots, issuing the orders. I got off on watching a strong woman obey. I got rock-hard at making such a powerful woman submit to me, giving her body as well as her heart.

So fucking hard.

The doors opened, and I stepped into her penthouse. It was quiet and she was nowhere in sight, so I knew she had followed my directions. I pulled my shirt over my head as I crossed the living room. I kicked off my shoes next as I kept moving. I turned into the bedroom and found her exactly as I imagined, holding her body up with one arm while two fingers were buried in her ass. A bottle of lube lay on the sheets beside her. She breathed hard, stretching herself for me with obvious enjoyment.

I stared at her luscious ass as my fingers undid my belt and jeans. Silky fair skin and slender fingers. A perfect back arched and toned. Her dark hair settled between her shoulder blades.

My jeans and boxers hit the floor, and that's when she heard me. She looked at me over her shoulder.

My cock was thicker than it'd ever been. Just when Titan had me at a new level of arousal, she exceeded it. I'd never forget the sight of this gorgeous woman fingering herself so I could fuck her tiny asshole with my enormous cock. Last time I fucked her in the ass, it hurt. But I'd have to get her used to it—because I really enjoyed it. Other women asked me to fuck them in the ass, but that was only because they thought I wanted it. The kinkier they were, the more likely it was that I would stick around. I never cared for it. But with Titan...I wanted to fuck her every single way I could. "Fuck."

I moved onto the bed and positioned myself behind her, watching her fingers continue to work her little hole. I leaned over her and wrapped my arm around her chest. I moved my mouth to her ear, and I listened to her breathe hard as she continued to finger herself. I never told her to stop, so she better keep going. "Lubed up for me, baby?"

"Yes," she said with a heavy breath.

"Yes, *Boss Man*."

She stiffened under my words but didn't disobey me. "Yes...Boss Man."

I moved back and held myself on my knees. I clicked open the bottle of lube and poured it all over my dick. The second I wrapped my hand around myself and I massaged the oil into my skin, I moaned. My cock was sensitive because I was so hard in anticipation. I tossed the bottle aside then grabbed her wrist before I pulled her hand away. Her ass was stretched and ready for me, slick with the lubrication. I took myself by the base and pushed inside her.

My entry was a lot easier than last time.

I moved in slowly, feeling the profound tightness from every direction. She squeezed my dick aggressively, and I felt it twitch in pleasure. It was perfect just like last time. The view was incredible and my fat dick was happy.

She moaned at my entrance, both in pleasure and pain. She arched her back harder and took heavy breaths as she accommodated my immense size in her petite channel. I wasn't even completely burrowed inside her, and she was struggling.

I moved farther until I was sheathed to the hilt.

She moaned again, hissing through her teeth as she combated the pain.

I had Tatum Titan on all fours, my big dick in her beautiful ass. I was a lucky son of a bitch. My hands gripped her hips as I prepared to fuck her. They slid up her waist to her tits, and I palmed both of them aggressively before I reached up and grabbed her by the back of the hair. "I've been thinking about this all day." I wrapped her hair around my knuckles until I had a perfect grip.

She continued to breathe heavily.

I started to move, giving it to her slow in the beginning. I needed her to relax, to take my cock gently so it wouldn't hurt her. But every time I thrust, my body just wanted to thrust harder. I wanted to fuck her viciously, to pound into that ass with the same aggression I fucked her pussy.

Somehow, I restrained myself.

Her moans became louder and she rocked back with

me, matching my gentle pace. She sheathed my cock over and over, her tiny asshole stretched wide apart.

I already wanted to come.

I started to move faster because I couldn't restrain myself. She breathed and moaned as she took me over and over.

I tugged on her hair and forced her face up to the ceiling. Like a puppet, she was completely under my control. I had her exactly where I wanted her, taking her in a way no other man ever had.

Fuck, I wanted to come.

My other hand moved to her clit, and I massaged her aggressively, needing to make her come fast because I wouldn't last. I worked her clit with my large fingers, feeling the wetness that had oozed from her pussy. I couldn't touch her like this without moving faster, so I fucked her harder than I did before.

She came quickly.

Thank god.

Her ass tightened as she came, and her entire body tensed as the euphoria swept over her. She clawed at the sheets, bucked her hips, and said my name in the midst of screams. When her moans died away and her ass loosened again, I knew she was finished.

I did the gentlemanly thing by allowing her to come first.

Now I was going to come in her ass.

I gripped both of her hips and pounded into her hard. The headboard smacked into the wall, and she moaned loudly as I took her roughly. In less than ten seconds, I hit my trigger and burst deep inside her ass.

Fucking incredible.

I gave her everything I had, depositing every drop I could inside her. I wanted it to sit there all night long, so a piece of me would always be with her. I let my cock soften inside her, feeling the phantom shots of pleasure. When I completely descended from my high, I pulled out of her.

I leaned over and pressed kisses along her spine, slightly apologetic for fucking her so ruthlessly. I loved this woman deeply, but my carnal instincts only seemed to intensify. There were times when I wanted to make love to her, to take my time and make her feel incredible with my touches and kisses.

But times like these, I just wanted to fuck her.

MY ARMS WERE SECURE AROUND HER WAIST, AND I PLACED kisses at the back of her neck as she stood under the running water. Drops splashed across her beautiful skin, and I licked them away with my tongue. Her audible breaths were nonexistent because the falling water drowned out the sound.

My hands explored her body like I'd never touched her before. My caresses were loving, an apology for the way I'd gripped her so violently before. I still wanted to remain in charge, but now I just wanted to feel her.

Kiss her.

Touch her.

Love her.

She turned around and faced me, the water hitting the back of her hair and washing away the conditioner. When her makeup was washed away and her hair was flat, she didn't look like the same executive in charge of a multibillion-dollar company. She just looked like a woman, a soft and beautiful one. I adored her authoritative fire, but her subtle simmer was equally as fascinating to me.

She was gorgeous.

My hand moved to her neck, and I could feel her gentle pulse throbbing against my fingertip. She was calm, her heart rate slow and peaceful. I liked to feel the life in her veins. I liked to feel her moods when she was with me. Once my lips were on her skin, her body kicked into overdrive. But when we experienced a quiet moment together, like this one, she was perfectly comfortable.

I stepped under the water, fisted her wet hair, and kissed her.

I was satisfied from fucking her so fiercely. She was satisfied with my performance.

But I always wanted more.

I wished I could have all of her.

I tasted the water on her mouth when our tongues danced together. The water cascaded down both of our bodies, enclosing us in a hiding place where no one would ever find us. Her plump, soft lips felt erotic against mine. I could kiss her forever. I'd never kissed a woman this way in my entire life. I didn't just feel arousal with her, but overwhelming passion. I constantly wanted more even though I'd already taken everything. Her heart rate quickened, and my breathing escalated. Her body was molded to mine, her soft tits pressing against my hard chest. Her nipples hardened against me. I could feel the tips as they puckered. My muscular arms wrapped around her petite frame, and I squeezed her tighter against me.

Minutes passed and it continued. I didn't have an end game in mind with this. I wouldn't mind making love to her, but that wasn't my goal. I just wanted to kiss her, to enjoy her. I wanted to feel her in my arms, to feel her shiver at my touch.

Being in love did crazy things to me. It turned me into a different man. It softened my hard edges. It changed my priorities. Money and power didn't seem so important anymore, not unless it made my woman happy. I'd wanted to rule this world alone, but once I'd met the perfect queen, I realized I wanted to share the throne with someone else.

I sucked her bottom lip into my mouth before I finally ended the embrace. My eyes looked into hers, seeing the same love that was burning in my heart. Her passion matched mine, if not exceeded it. I would do anything for this woman, and I knew she would do anything for me. No matter what the outside world did to either of us, we were always loyal to each other. Nothing could shake our commitment to one another. Even when she questioned my motives and struggled to trust me, she still had my back.

That was real love.

I cupped both of her cheeks and brushed my nose against hers. "I love you." Maybe it was something I shouldn't say since she had committed to Thorn, but I didn't give a damn. A real man didn't hide his feelings for the woman he loved. Whether she could handle it or not, I was going to speak my mind. I was looking at the most amazing woman in the world, and my heart was singing.

Her eyes shifted back and forth as she looked into mine, and she didn't surround herself with any walls. She remained vulnerable to me, connected to me as we stood under the running water. When we were away from the public, we were bound together even more tightly. Our love was uninterrupted. "I love you too."

I pressed my forehead to hers and closed my eyes, feeling the undeniable connection between us. It was difficult to see her during the day, both of us dressed in our expensive clothes with executive pretenses, when all I wanted to do was be real with her. When I walked into her office, the first thing I wanted to do was kiss her. When reporters snooped into my personal life, I wanted to tell them I was in love with Tatum Titan. When I went out with the guys, I wanted to wear a band on my left hand so women wouldn't waste their time with me. I wanted to be transparent with my affection, wear my heart on my sleeve.

One day I would have that. I just had to be patient.

We got out of the shower, dried off, and then got into bed. I was in my boxers, and she pulled out one of my t-shirts from the drawer. It must have been one I left behind because I didn't remember giving it to her.

It looked better on her than it did on me anyway.

I lay beside her in bed and hooked her leg over my waist. Face-to-face on the pillow, we stared at each other. I hadn't slept through the night with her in months. It used to be a regular occurrence, but now those days were over.

I missed them.

I didn't bother trying to stick around anymore either. She always asked me to leave, and that routinely pissed me off. That left things on bad terms, and I hated ending things that way every night. "You're damn beautiful, you know that."

Her eyes softened the same way they always did when I gave her an unexpected compliment. Her hand rested against my chest, and she brushed her palm against the hard muscles of my pectorals. "You're sweet."

"Just honest. Sometimes that makes me sweet. Sometimes it makes me an asshole."

"You're never an asshole to me."

"Because you're beautiful." My fingers explored her waistline underneath her t-shirt.

"I think there's more to it than that..."

I kissed the corner of her mouth. "Because I'm in love with you."

Her eyes softened again.

I knew I was making the evening intense with my confessions, but I wasn't going to downplay my feelings for this woman. All I could do was change the subject. "How'd it go with Kyle?"

Her fingers brushed across my skin to the center of my sternum. "He came by the office this afternoon. We sat down for a few hours and discussed our options."

"And did you feel good about it?"

"I did," she whispered. "He can give me exactly what I want, and I can give him exactly what he wants. He didn't mention Vincent, which was a relief. I wouldn't have known what to say to him if he had."

"Nothing to discuss."

"So we're moving forward. It would be nice to get in everywhere that Vincent mentioned, but I'm just glad to start somewhere. It's always been one of my biggest goals. If it weren't for you, it wouldn't be happening."

My thumb swiped across her belly button. "It would still happen. Just not right now."

A warm smile spread across her lips. "This deal was really important to me...thank you for making it happen."

"My father can fuck with me, but he can't fuck with you." And he would definitely be coming after me soon enough. Kyle probably turned down his offer just a few hours ago. He was probably gripping the edge of his desk with his teeth on edge.

She explored my hard stomach with her fingertips, feeling the grooves in between the muscles. She loved the strength of my body, the way I was packed with muscle but without fat. I had a protein shake for breakfast, a protein-packed salad for lunch, and I hit the gym every day. I didn't care that much about my health. But I cared about making her legs shake when I was buried deep inside her.

She eyed my body with a lustful expression in her gaze. Her fingertips trailed farther down until she found the outline of my cock through my boxers. She rubbed her fingers along my length and gave my shaft a gentle squeeze before she rolled me to my back. She climbed on top of me, pulled down my shorts to expose my length, and then inserted my dick inside her.

I lay back and gripped her hips, enjoying her slick pussy as much as I had that tight asshole. I loved fucking her, but I loved it when she took me when she felt like it. She knew exactly what she wanted, and she wasn't afraid to make her intentions known. She rode my dick like a pro, her eyes locked on me.

I was definitely a lucky man.

4

TITAN

"Maybe we should have the wedding on Martha's Vineyard," Liv, Thorn's mother, said. "It's so beautiful there. Thomas and I go every summer when the flowers are at their finest."

"Not a bad idea," Thomas said. "Or we do a beach wedding. Everyone likes those."

I drank my wine and looked out the window to see people passing in their heavy coats. The restaurant was warm, with fireplaces spaced around the room. Dates enjoyed each other's company over candlelight and a nice bottle of wine. The distant sound of forks tapping against the plates filled the room. The conversation carried on, but I didn't focus my attention on it. I thought about a lot of things, like my new relationship with Kyle Livingston, what Vincent Hunt would do in retaliation, and what my lover was doing right now...Diesel Hunt. Every time he said he loved me, I immediately said it back. Every time he kissed me, I kissed him back harder.

"I don't care where we get married." Thorn had his arm draped over the back of my chair. He didn't directly touch me, but he was deeply affectionate whenever we were in public. Now that we were engaged, he touched me more often. For most of the evening, his hand had rested on my thigh. He was in slacks and a dark blue collared shirt, his powerful physique stretching the fabric in masculine ways. "I just care about the honeymoon."

Thomas laughed at his son's crude comment.

Liv smiled then covered up her smirk with a sip of her wine.

I was only partially paying attention.

"What are your thoughts?" Liv asked, her gaze directed at me.

I quickly swallowed my wine and tried to pretend I'd been engaged in the conversation the entire time. "I wouldn't mind something simple. All I really care about is the dress. An outdoor wedding would be preferable." This was the only wedding I would ever have, so I should put more effort into it. Our children would see pictures someday. But it was hard for me to get truly excited when we weren't in love. I wouldn't question Thorn's happiness or mine on the big day because I knew we loved each other so deeply, but I knew that love would never be passionate...not like the kind I had with Hunt.

"Then it should be on Martha's Vineyard," Liv said. "What do you think?"

That sounded fine enough. "Sure. What do you think, Thorn?"

He shrugged. "Like I said, I only care about the honeymoon." His wineglass was empty, so he helped himself to mine.

If we were alone, I'd swat his hand away.

"Then it's settled," Liv said. "I know of a great wedding planner out there who can help us out." She looked like a springtime flower that was blooming after a cold winter. She was over the moon that her eldest son was getting married. He was the first one in the family to do it. "We need to work on your wedding dress next."

"I'll talk to Connor Suede about it," I said. "I'm sure he could design something wonderful."

Thorn nodded in agreement. "He really understands how to highlight your natural beauty." He turned to me with a handsome smile.

"Thanks," I said.

Liv smiled at the two of us. "You guys are so great together. Sometimes you just know when two people are going to be together for the rest of their lives."

Thorn and I hadn't even kissed each other, and we spent our time in bed with other people. But we did have a powerful connection between us. Even if we never married, he would always be a significant person in my life. To me, he was family. "I think so too."

"What about kids?" his mother pressed. "That's happening soon, right?"

"Liv," Thomas said quietly. "Let them get married first and see how it goes..."

Liv looked slightly embarrassed but couldn't cover up her excitement.

Thorn addressed it. "We want to have kids pretty soon. Titan feels like she's getting old, and I'm ready to start a family."

Liv looked like the happiest mother in the world. "Oh...that's so wonderful." She covered her mouth with her hands as tears sprung in her eyes.

Thomas smiled, unable to hide his excitement. "Well, you know that makes us very happy."

I was grateful my kids would have wonderful grandparents. Thorn's parents were very sweet. They were a little too involved in Thorn's life, but that wasn't necessarily a bad thing. I didn't have any relatives, so I was glad my kids would have a strong family of grandparents and uncles.

"So right after the wedding, then?" Liv asked.

"Pretty much." Thorn turned to me with a grin on his face. "Maybe we'll start on the honeymoon."

"Maybe." That didn't sound like a bad idea. The

whole reason we were getting married was so I could start our family. No reason to wait.

Thorn winked. "This trip is gonna be awesome."

KYLE SAT ACROSS FROM ME IN THE CONFERENCE ROOM AT Stratosphere. "China is the biggest retailer in the world. America comes in a close second, but in terms of actual items sold, it's further down the list. But since the prices are much higher elsewhere, that's why they compete so well."

"I agree."

"I think we should start your products in the high-end stores and market them as luxury items. Beauty is a big deal for a lot of women there, and they want the best product out there. But we'll have to redo the label to serve this demographic better. While it's sleek and elegant for the American market, it clashes with the Chinese audience."

"Makes sense. I can have my team put something together."

"I was actually thinking my team would come up with something," he said. "Since we work in that space a lot. How about I bring it to you and ask for your opinion, then we can go from there? I assumed you would be handling my marketing as well since you understand this field so much better than I do."

That was fair. "I think it's a good plan."

"Awesome." He closed his tablet and organized his papers before he dropped them into his bag. "I think this is going to be a great partnership. Hunt speaks so highly of you, which is strange because he doesn't seem to have anything nice to say about anyone."

I smiled as I rose to my feet. "He's a bit grouchy sometimes."

Kyle chuckled and walked with me to the door. "There's obviously something about you that doesn't make him grouchy."

We walked to the lobby where our four assistants were working, taking phone calls and working on spreadsheets.

"Do you know who his mystery woman is, by the way?" Kyle stopped walking as he adjusted his satchel over his shoulder.

Right at that moment, the elevator doors opened and Hunt emerged, looking sleek and deadly in his black suit with his matching hair. He stepped onto the floor like owned the whole building, not just half of it. His eyes were only on me, as if Kyle and the four assistants weren't even there.

As always, my heart soared like a bird that just took flight.

"I'm sorry, I don't," I said to Kyle. "Hunt and I don't discuss our personal lives."

"That doesn't surprise me." Kyle turned to Hunt when he approached us. "Hunt." He shook his hand.

Hunt reciprocated before he placed his hands in his pockets. "Business going well?"

"It is," Kyle said. "You were right about Titan. She's got an incredible mind."

It was nice to hear a compliment once in a while. Men were usually intimidated or annoyed by my success. They put me down rather than praised me. Maybe being associated with Hunt had changed people's perception of me. After Hunt declared war against Bruce Carol, the industry knew not to cross him. And since he did business with me...they shouldn't cross me either. I didn't need his shadow to protect me, but I'd be lying if I said it wasn't nice getting this kind of respect.

"She does." Hunt turned his gaze on me. As if Kyle weren't standing right there, he gave me that typical possessive look. He clearly didn't give a damn if anyone picked up on it.

If Kyle paid a little more attention, he would have the answer to the question he'd just asked me.

"I'll see you later." Kyle shook my hand before he walked away. "Having lunch with the wife before the kids get out of school."

"Enjoy your alone time while you can," I said.

"Will do." He waved then got into the elevator.

Hunt and I stepped into the conference room, and he shut the door behind us even though I preferred to keep it open. Anytime we were in public but not visible, I was high-strung. Hunt didn't respect boundaries. If anything, he wanted to be caught in the act.

I purposely moved to the other side of the table so there would be a solid barrier in between us.

He stood with his hands in pockets, his heavy gaze centered right on me. When he was dressed like that, sexy in all black, it was hard not to think about stripping everything off and throwing it to the floor. Images of us in bed together came to mind, the sweat, the moans, the orgasms...like they were plastered on a TV screen. I couldn't be close to him without sex crossing my mind. I couldn't touch him without thinking about the way he told me he loved me.

My brain turned into a fried egg.

He watched me like he was witnessing all of those thoughts for himself.

Maybe we needed to screw every morning and every night so these tense encounters wouldn't happen anymore. Or maybe they would just make us want each other more. Judging by the shameless way he eye-fucked me, it probably wouldn't make a difference.

"You look beautiful today." He could get any woman on her back if he just said those words. He could walk up to her in a bar, not even bother introducing himself, and she'd be on her knees sucking him off in the bathroom.

"We aren't doing that."

A grin crept onto his lips. "Then how did it go with Kyle?"

"Really well. We made a lot of progress."

"Good." His grin didn't change. "And I still think you look beautiful today."

I did my best to glare at him, but it was a pathetic attempt. "What happened to professionalism?"

"I'm not touching you, am I?"

Only because the table was between us. "Kyle and I are going to work on rebranding next. It'll be a few months before we can start testing products in our territories, but at least we're going somewhere."

"These things take time. I'm glad you guys are getting along so well."

"He's very nice. I feel like people have been a lot nicer to me in general since we started working together."

He dropped his smile, turning serious. "People know they shouldn't piss me off."

I crossed my arms over my chest and made sure I stuck to my side of the table. If a piece of furniture weren't in the way, I could imagine my hands moving up and down his chest. A soft kiss sounded perfect for lunch. I wouldn't mind hiking up my skirt for a quickie. I could bend over the table, and he could ram me from behind. Then his come would be sitting inside me for the rest of the day.

Wow, I needed to get my shit together.

Hunt regarded me with that ferocious stare, like the table wouldn't get in his way if he really wanted to grab me.

Now my knees were getting weak.

My breath was coming out unevenly.

I almost didn't care that we were at work.

He obviously didn't.

"If we're done here, I'll see you later." I had to dismiss him now. Otherwise, my panties would be around my ankles.

"You're going to have to come around the table sometime."

I stayed put. "I have a few things to do here."

He called my bluff with a smile. "Whatever you say, Titan." He stepped out of the room and turned around at the door.

I stared at his fine ass in his slacks. It was tight and muscular. I wanted to sink my teeth into it then and there.

He turned around before he stepped out. "I have dinner plans tonight, just so you know."

My heart fell with disappointment. He'd come over every night this week. "Oh..."

"I'll be home at eight...if you want to surprise me."
He walked out and let the door shut behind him.

He was so arrogant, and it drove me crazy.

But I knew I would be there at eight.

He knew it too.

I WAS READY FOR HIM WHEN THE ELEVATOR DOORS OPENED.
I was in my black teddy and garters, along with shiny
black heels. My hair was curled the way he liked, and my
makeup was dark and heavy. Seeing him in that black suit
had driven me crazy all day. I couldn't stop thinking about
having him, about taking him deep and hard. It was as if I
hadn't been enjoying him every single night of the week.

He was still in the black suit he wore earlier today,
looking handsome and sexy. His jaw was cleanly shaven,
his hair was still neat, and he didn't look the least bit
surprised to see me waiting for him.

As he walked closer to me, his smile widened. His
eyes roamed over my body in the sultry lingerie, and a
lustful look of approval was in his eyes. He slowly peeled
off his jacket and tossed it on the floor, as if the expensive
coat didn't mean a damn thing to him. His eyes never left
my face.

"Hands by your sides."

He hesitated before he obeyed.

My fingers worked the buttons of his shirt. I yanked the tie off and placed it over my shoulder to use later. His belt was undone and his fly was open. I pushed all of his clothes to the floor, enjoying the spectacular view of his body as more skin was revealed. When he was naked in front of me, all muscle with a fat cock between his legs, I moved into him and kissed his chest. My tongue explored the hard muscles until I sucked one of his nipples into his mouth.

He watched me lustfully and dug one hand into my hair.

I shoved his arm down and kept kissing him. I slid down to my knees so I was level with his throbbing cock. My mouth opened, and I took his large length down my throat. When he face-fucked me, it made my throat raw and my tear ducts sting. But it felt so good at the same time. I slathered his entire shaft with my saliva and sucked the tip so I could taste the pre-come he had already begun to release.

He fought the urge to touch me by keeping his hands by his sides. But he watched me with a powerful look of desperation. A masculine moan emerged from deep in his throat, the most erotic sound I'd ever heard.

I soaked him with my mouth before I rose to my feet again. Giving head was something I could do all day when it came to Diesel Hunt, but I had bigger plans in mind. I wanted to get on that gorgeous body and please myself.

I already had a kitchen chair placed in the middle of the floor, and he knew exactly what it was for. "Sit."

His eyes were trained on my lips, so he leaned down to kiss me.

I pulled away, making him miss the mark. "*Sit.*"

My movement seemed to amuse him more than annoy him because he smiled before he followed my directions. He seated his massive body in the chair, his long legs open as his dick rested against his stomach. His hand wrapped around his length, and he rubbed himself slowly as he watched me. "What are you going to do to me, baby?"

I pushed his arms back so they dangled past the chair. "Everything." I undid the crotch in my teddy before I climbed onto the chair. "No touching."

He growled loudly.

I planted my feet on the chair then gripped his massive shoulders for balance. I wanted to fuck him the way I wanted to, to use him as a gorgeous man rather than someone I loved. I pointed his cock at my entrance then slowly slid down.

I was wet before he even came home.

I pushed down to the bottom and breathed through the pleasure.

He moaned too, both of his hands formed into fists.

"I could barely keep my hands off you today." I slowly moved up and down, my fingertips digging into his powerful muscle. He stretched me apart every time he was deep inside me. My pussy loved the sensation of utter fullness. Hunt was a man who always felt incredible—every time.

"Then you shouldn't have." His look intensified, and he became darker and more brooding. His intensity was exceptional, enough to nearly suffocate me. His hands still didn't touch me, but his arms began to shake from the force of his restraint. "You should have bent over that table, hiked up your skirt, and told me to fuck you."

My pussy tightened around his dick in response. "I'd rather save it for tonight."

"I wouldn't. I want both." His feet pushed against the floor, and he thrust up into me. He wanted more of my pussy than I was giving him.

"No." I stopped moving, making him stationary.

He growled in my face.

"I'm fucking you the way I want. You're supposed to sit there and let me."

His eyes darkened as he looked at me. "Yes, Boss Lady."

My arms circled his neck, and I kept moving at the pace I enjoyed. I liked long and even strokes. I liked getting his fatness at a slow tempo in the beginning.

Once my body lit on fire, I would squat at a quicker pace. "Your cock feels so good…"

His hands slid up my thighs, and he used his strength to help me move up and down. He had powerful arms, so he lightened the load on my glutes and hamstrings. He kneaded my ass with his fingertips at the same time. Then he spanked me.

A moan escaped my lips.

He spanked me again when he knew I liked it.

I scooted closer to him so I could take his entire length with every thrust. I wanted to swat his hands away, but with his help, I could fuck him harder. He was hitting me in the perfect spot over and over, and I was already biting my lip in enjoyment.

"Come all over my dick, baby." He looked me in the eye, his expression scorching and sexy.

After a few more pumps, I was there. I was grinding on his dick at a faster tempo, and I was experiencing a blinding orgasm that made me scream right in his face. I clawed at his back and nearly drew blood as I enjoyed my high. Hunt was the only man I liked to use so much. He satisfied me a fix no other man ever could. I knew I wanted him to be the man I fucked for the rest of my life. I didn't want anyone else, just him.

When I opened my eyes, he was looking at me. His jaw was tense and his expression was tenser.

I knew he was about to come. "Not until I say so."

He released a scoff along with a slight smile. "I shouldn't have expected anything else, Boss Lady."

THORN SAT ACROSS FROM ME AT THE TABLE IN HIS NAVY blue suit. A black tie ran down his chest, and a shiny watch sat on his wrist. He was a hard man with a body thick like concrete. His facial features were masculine and handsome, but they had a slight softness to them. Pilar described him as a pretty boy. With dirty-blond hair and blue eyes, he was much fairer than Hunt's darkness.

We met for lunch in the middle of the workday, talking about work and the wedding. A gorgeous woman walked by in a tight skirt and a low-cut blouse, and she was distracting enough that I even noticed her.

Thorn didn't even glance. His eyes remained on me the entire time.

"Did you not see her?" I asked incredulously.

He shrugged and drank his Old Fashioned.

"Are you okay?" This wasn't the Thorn I knew. Thorn had wandering eyes and definitely a wandering dick.

"Come on," he said as he put his glass down. "You're my fiancée. I'm not gonna stare at another woman's ass when you're sitting across from me."

I cocked my eyebrow. "Because...?" I didn't care what he did during his personal time, and he certainly didn't care what I did in the privacy of my bedroom. "You're afraid someone will see you?"

"Yes. But it's also rude."

"How do you figure?"

He drank from his glass again before he licked his lips. "You're going to be my wife. Even if we aren't in love, I still love and respect you. When we're together, you're the only woman on my mind. You're my primary focus. You're gonna be the mother of my kids. You won't have my fidelity, but you'll have everything else. I still want to be a husband to you."

My eyes softened because I'd never expected Thorn to say something like that.

"I would hope the same from you," he said quietly. "After all, it's the two of us against the world. Women will come and go...but we're in this together forever. So you're my priority, and I'd better be yours."

"You know, that's the most romantic thing I've ever heard you say."

"Yeah?" he asked with a smile. "Hmm...I guess it is. Never thought I was the romantic type."

"That makes two of us. But I see your reasoning."

"Besides, I don't want my kids to see my checking out some other woman, you know? I want them to know we love each other and we're happy. The last thing I would want is for them to think I'm a cheater. I suspect they would never understand the parameters of our relationship, even as adults."

"No, probably not."

He finished his drink then leaned farther over the table, his elbows on the surface. "So, is Martha's Vineyard okay? Or were you just saying what my mother wanted to hear?"

"It doesn't make a difference to me. What do you want?"

"Whatever you want," he said. "This is your big day."

"You know I'd like to just get hitched somewhere and get it over with."

He grinned. "True."

"The only thing I'm looking forward to is getting a dress."

"You'll look stunning. I'm actually looking forward to taking it off you." He gave me a heated expression, similar to the kind Hunt gave me.

All we'd ever done was hold hands or kiss each other on the cheek. I'd never even kissed him on the mouth. Going from platonic friends to lovers would be strange. "How is this going to work?"

"Your meaning?" We sat at a small table near the back of the restaurant. People were gathered around us, but we had enough space that we weren't overheard.

"You and I will always have other partners, so how do

we take care of our sexual health? Do we get tested every time?"

"I guess so."

"Because that would become tedious…"

"Yeah, you're right." He rubbed his jawline as he considered it. "I guess we could wear a condom."

"But I'm monogamous in my relationships."

"But you aren't always in a relationship. There's usually months in between, right?"

"True."

"Then we should be fine. And during those windows, I'm not wearing a condom. It'll be a nice change." He locked his gaze with me, unashamed by his intentions.

"You don't think it'll be weird?" I asked honestly.

"Not really," he said simply. "You're a very attractive woman, Titan. I'm great in the sack. I think it'll be easy for both of us. Don't overthink it."

None of this had bothered me until Hunt walked into my life. Now I felt guilty for even thinking about kissing Thorn. It felt strange to imagine myself having sex with him when I was spending all my nights with Hunt.

Thorn caught the unease on my face. "Hunt?"

He read my expression like an open book. "I've been sleeping with him for a long time now."

"That fire will burn out anyway. They always do." He waved the waiter over so he could order another drink.

He hit the whiskey again even though it was only a little past noon. "How are things with him?"

"About the same."

"And what does the same mean?" He stirred his drink before he brought the glass to his lips.

"It's just sex now. We don't talk as much anymore."

Thorn nodded. "I wondered what would happen after we got engaged."

"We didn't talk for over a week. But he came back around, a little hostile. It's been getting easier ever since."

"Maybe he's finally given up."

Hunt still told me he loved me, said it with such meaning that I lost my grasp of reality. He touched me delicately as he whispered those words to me, his affection washing over me like his warm breath. "Yeah...maybe."

The waitress brought our lunch, two garden salads with no dressing. Thorn added extra chicken to his so he would get enough protein for the day. He was as obsessed with his diet as he was with making money.

"I don't think I told you the good news."

He finished chewing before he spoke. "What good news?"

"Kyle Livingston and I have partnered up."

Thorn cared about food more than anything else—almost. But he ignored his lunch and stared at me in shock. "When did this happen?"

"Earlier this week."

"Vincent Hunt never made good on his word?" He wiped his mouth with a napkin and set down his fork.

"No, he did. But Kyle didn't take the offer."

Thorn's eyebrows practically popped off his head. "Why the hell not?"

"Hunt talked him out it. Said Kyle should work with me instead."

"Seriously? And it worked?"

I nodded. "I'm not entirely sure what he said to Kyle, but he basically said Kyle believed in my partnership more than Hunt's father's. He said I had a lot to offer and Vincent wasn't trustworthy. Hunt somehow used his influence to talk Kyle out of a deal of a lifetime."

"Jesus..." Thorn sat back in his chair, still floored by the revelation. "This changes everything."

"I know. Kyle and I have already gotten off to a great start. He's easy to work with, and he respects me."

"He'd better," Thorn snapped. "If he did otherwise, I'd make his life a living hell."

I smiled at his protectiveness, my future husband immediately turning in a guard dog. "Anyway, Hunt made it happen."

He slowly nodded as his eyes shifted away. A quiet sigh left his lips, and his shoulders straightened as he considered what I'd said. His eyes then landed on something interesting because his pupils immediately contracted. "Speaking of the devil..."

I turned my head to see Hunt enter the restaurant with a gorgeous brunette leading the way. She was in a tight black dress, matching heels, and a pink wallet. Black frames sat on the bridge of her nose, making her look smart and sexy.

Like any other instance when I saw him with an attractive woman, I felt sick to my stomach. I was far too confident in myself to ever feel jealous or threatened, but with Hunt, all my suave coolness evaporated. I was uneasy and unnerved. I tried not to stare, but I couldn't help but be irritated by the sight of her. There was an explanation for this, so I just had to stay calm.

They reached their table, and Hunt pulled out the chair for her like a perfect gentleman.

The sickness was getting worse.

Thorn eyed them before he shifted his expression back to me.

I knew exactly what he was thinking.

"One moment, he helps you out with a great business deal. And then the next moment...he's having lunch with a gorgeous woman." He shook his head. "Just like old times."

Sweat collected on my chest, and I felt my breathing escalate. Hunt spent all of his evenings in bed with me, so I found it hard to believe he had time for anyone else.

When he told me he loved me, it seemed like those words were coming from the bottom of his heart. I wanted to give him the benefit of the doubt because I didn't want to be played so fiercely.

Hunt sat perfectly straight in his gray suit, his musculature obvious even through his clothing. He wore a black watch, shiny dress shoes, and he stared at her head on with a serious expression. They seemed to be in the midst of an intense conversation, which didn't bode well either.

I might hurl everything I just ate.

"Let's stop by and say hello." Thorn placed his napkin on the table.

"I'm not doing that."

"Come on. We can catch him when he least expects it."

"No. Even if he is sneaking around, I'm not going to march over there and act like a crazy jealous woman."

"You won't. Just be cool."

I drank my water. "Forget it."

Thorn turned back to them. "Then I guess we'll just watch what happens."

———

THEY TALKED ALL THROUGH LUNCH. NOT A SINGLE TOUCH transpired through the conversation. He didn't rest his hand on hers on the table. If he did, I probably would have lost my shit.

Thorn and I were long finished with our lunch, but we kept ordering drinks just to stall.

I felt pathetic lurking around so I could watch Hunt.

I hated not trusting him. I missed the days when I didn't think twice about what he was doing. I could see him with a beautiful woman and not even consider the possibility he was two-timing me. The trust was ironclad. But once I'd seen a photograph of him kissing some woman, we hadn't gained back everything we'd lost.

"I'm not sure what to make of it," Thorn said as he kept staring at them.

"Maybe they're just colleagues."

"That woman is drop-dead sexy. Yeah, right."

I glared at him. "You aren't making me feel better."

"It's not my job to make you feel better. It's my job to tell you what you don't want to hear." He eyed them again. "And if I saw that woman in a bar, I'd be buying all of her drinks until she was in my sheets."

If Thorn thought she was sexy, then Hunt must have thought the same thing. But I shouldn't let that bother me so much. I should remain confident like I'd always been not to feel threatened by it. I kept drinking my water, but I wished I had something stronger.

They both stood from the table.

Thank god. It was finally over.

Thorn raised his hand in the air and whistled.

I slammed my drink down. "What the hell are you doing?"

Hunt turned in our direction and stilled when he saw us. The woman did as well.

This couldn't be happening.

Thorn waved him over. "I caught him with his pants down. We'll see how he plays this."

"I hate you so much right now," I whispered.

"Hate you too, sweetheart," he said with a grin.

Hunt led the way, one hand in his pocket with his typically stoic expression. He didn't seem alarmed at all by our presence, even if we'd been watching him the entire time. He arrived at the table with the woman beside him. "Thorn." He extended his hand.

Thorn shook it, his smile gone. "Hunt."

He turned to me next but didn't shake my hand. "Titan." Instead of touching me, he greeted me with an intense expression he never showed to anyone else. Whether we were in a crowded room or not, he looked at me like I belonged to him and no one else. The ring on my finger meant nothing to him.

I didn't say anything back.

Hunt indicated the woman beside him. "This is McKenzie." He introduced her to the both of us.

I shook her hand but loathed every second of it. I ignored her beaming smile and the way her hair perfectly settled around her shoulders when she stood upright again.

Hunt continued to behave naturally. "McKenzie is one of my top candidates to head my HR department. This was her second interview."

It was a job interview.

Oh, thank god.

I nearly clutched my chest in relief.

McKenzie nodded. "It was a pleasure to meet you both of you."

Hunt didn't say goodbye, but he gave me that a scorching expression before he turned away and walked out with McKenzie. He didn't place his hand on the small of her back the way he did with me. His hands always remained in his pockets, nowhere near this woman he just interviewed.

When they were gone, it was just the two of us again.

"Well, I feel better," Thorn said.

"Yeah, I do too." Except I didn't want to picture him working with her on a regular basis.

Thorn grinned. "Still jealous?"

"I'm not jealous," I lied.

He chuckled. "You can lie to Hunt, and he'll probably believe you. But you can't lie to me." He winked. "Don't worry. I'll keep your secret."

I covered my frown by drinking my water.

5

HUNT

I STEPPED onto the top floor of Stratosphere and made my way into Titan's office. She sat behind her desk, her hands perfectly aligned on the keyboard with her eyes directed at the screen. She finished her email even after I stepped into the room and took a seat.

I crossed my legs and looked over my portfolio as I waited. No one ever made me wait, but Titan wasn't the kind of woman who waited for anyone either.

I loved that about her.

She finished before she turned to me. "How's your day?"

"Good. Yours?" Just a few hours ago, she'd spotted me with one of my most competitive applicants. McKenzie was a Harvard graduate who'd had a year-long internship at a respectable software company. Her grades were impressive, and her demeanor was exceptional. I could see her leading an entire building of workers and handling complicated cases.

When I'd looked at Titan in that restaurant, I knew she was uncomfortable. She didn't trust me, feared I was on a date with McKenzie. It pissed me off that she thought so little of me, that I would be fucking her every night but still run off with another woman behind her back. I reminded myself I needed to be understanding due to our sensitive situation, but that didn't dim my annoyance.

Like I could ever want another woman but Titan.

Ridiculous.

Titan took a minute to answer my question. "It's been long."

I didn't bring up our earlier encounter, and I knew she wouldn't either. There wasn't anything to say. I could point out her obvious jealousy, but it seemed like a moot point. I started from the beginning and discussed the figures for this past week. We'd just launched our holiday marketing program, and all the retailers were shifting to meet our needs.

We went back and forth for forty-five minutes straight. Titan was always to be on top of things even though she seemed busier than I was. Her insights were genius, and she could juggle a huge amount of information without getting things confused. She did all of it with a smooth persona, never giving any indication she was stressed. In fact, she seemed almost bored.

She was an excellent businesswoman.

When we finished, there was nothing more to say. This was the time I excused myself to my office or I returned to my building. But I chose to sit there instead, spinning the pen in my fingertips as I watched her. My eyes roamed over her body, wishing I were looking at her naked instead of covered in designer clothes.

Titan met my look, her guard up high. "Yes?"

"I hope you felt stupid today." I'd thought I could swallow my anger, but it slipped out anyway.

She knew exactly what I meant, judging by the way her eyes narrowed. "I didn't. Thorn was the suspicious one."

"And you were the jealous one."

Instead of denying it, she flipped through the papers on her desk. "I have a lot of work to do, Hunt. I'll see you later."

"No reason to be jealous, Titan. You're the only woman I want. How many times do I have to tell you that?"

"Enough times to make me forget about that picture of you kissing that woman." She fired back with the same rage while keeping her voice at a low level.

I didn't explain the photograph because I already had a million times. I kept spinning the pen, giving my fingers something to do. "You shouldn't feel threatened by anyone, not when you're Titan."

"But Tatum is threatened by a gorgeous woman Thorn can't stop staring at," she countered. "And if he can't stop thinking about fucking her, then neither can you...not that I should care."

My eyes narrowed in offense. "That's not what I was thinking."

"Whatever, Hunt."

I wasn't lying. "I was thinking about her qualifications for the position."

"Whatever you say," she said dismissively.

If the desk weren't in the way, I'd grab her by the neck. I slammed my fist onto the wooden surface, making everything shake like an earthquake had struck. "Look at me."

She stilled at my violent reaction and shifted her gaze to mine.

"I won't hire her if that's what you want."

That seemed to piss her off more because she rose to her feet, trembling like she was about to launch her own earthquake.

I stood up, towering over her to ensure I had the upper hand.

"Don't insult me like that ever again."

"Insult you?" I asked, having no idea what pissed her off so much.

"If she's qualified for the position, you'd better hire her. Disqualifying her just because she's attractive is unacceptable. I wouldn't respect you for discriminating against someone over something so petty."

That was my girl.

"You understand me?"

I tried not to smile. I loved her pride, her feminism. She put aside her own jealousy because she knew she was being self-centered. She didn't directly admit her wrongdoing, but it was pretty much a confession. "Then I'm going to hire her."

"Good." She returned to her seat, shrugging off the conversation.

I remained on my feet and placed my hand against her desk, invading her space. "You want to know what I was thinking about when I was interviewing her?"

She wouldn't meet my gaze, pretending to read a document instead.

"I was thinking about texting you."

"To say what?" she whispered.

I leaned farther over the desk so my lips were near her ear. "That I missed you."

I DRANK FROM MY GLASS WHILE ONE HAND RESTED IN THE pocket of my tuxedo. Pine talked about the work he was doing with his father, pushing papers around and crunching numbers. When a beautiful woman walked by in a ball gown, his eyes always followed her until she was gone from sight.

I didn't notice any of them.

"How's work?" Pine asked.

"Same old shit." I didn't discuss business outside of work often. It seemed like a conflict of interest, and it was also boring.

"That can't be true if you've partnered up with Tatum Titan." He nudged me in the side.

"She's just like another executive."

"But she's hot."

My eyes shifted to him, a warning in my gaze.

"What?" he asked innocently. "You don't think she's hot?"

I thought she was damn hot, but I was the only person who had the right to say it out loud. "Don't talk about her like that."

"Geez, chill. Didn't mean any harm by it."

"Then just stop talking." I drank from my glass again. We were gathered together for a charity fundraiser. They'd asked me to give a speech since I was responsible for the largest charity donation of the year. I didn't do it for publicity, and now it was biting me in the ass.

Pine peered across the room. "There she is."

I'd been expecting her. She told me she was coming

with Thorn, and I gritted my teeth in silence. I didn't like seeing them together even if she spent all her nights with me. Just watching him hold her hand irritated me. He got to claim her for the world to see when it should have been me.

She wore a black dress with a deep cut in the back. It showed her spine all the way to the top of her ass. It highlighted the small muscles of her frame, her perfect posture, and her flawless skin. The steep curve of her back made her ass more prominent, and I'd have a hard time staring at it this evening. Her hair was pulled up in an elegant updo, allowing the skin of her neck to be revealed. I couldn't see her face because she was turned the other way. But I could see the way her dress reached the floor.

She looked like a queen.

Pine whistled under his breath. "Jesus Christ…"

My hand rested in my pocket, but it automatically tightened into a fist. "Be very careful, Pine."

He took my warning and swallowed his next words.

"Oh, shit."

"What?" I asked.

"Did you know your father was going to be here?"

My eyes moved to the doorway, and I saw him step inside in a black tuxedo. He greeted people at the door, wearing his charismatic smile. A woman in her twenties was on his arm, beautiful and exotic.

My father and I crossed paths rarely, and we pretended the other didn't exist. But this was the first time I'd seen him since he threatened me in my office. He wouldn't make a move toward me out in the open, but he wouldn't hide his hostility.

Tonight would be interesting.

THORN BECAME PREOCCUPIED TALKING TO HIS acquaintances, so I appeared at her side with a flute of champagne. "You look beautiful."

She dropped her smile momentarily when she realized I had joined her. She knew I would be there, so it couldn't have caught her off guard. She took the glass, looked into my eyes in a way she never looked at anyone else, and then took a drink. "Thank you."

I leaned down and kissed her on the cheek, taking my time feeling her skin with my lips. In a few hours, I'd be the one peeling off her dress and tasting her everywhere. Both of her nipples would be in my mouth, sucked until they were raw. My tongue would explore her folds and taste her arousal for me. I would make love to her for the night, convincing her she was the only woman who existed in my thoughts—and my heart.

She held her breath when I kissed her, feeling the wave of chemistry the instant we touched. We could both feel it as soon as we were in the same vicinity. I could take her breath away so easily. And she could bring me to my knees with the snap of a finger.

I pulled away, resisting the urge to wrap my arm around her petite waist. I wanted to drag my fingertips down her bare back, feel the smooth skin that my chest would soon be pressed against.

We stared at each for a solid minute. The crowd enjoyed their evening with good company and fine liquor. Laughter erupted in different areas, loud and fake. People passed us as they ventured to greet someone they recognized. We remained absolutely still, just looking at one another.

I savored the look of her red-painted lips. Her makeup was done heavily for the evening, creating sultry eyes, gorgeous cheekbones, and a plump mouth. It didn't matter how she dressed herself up or how she did her makeup. She looked beautiful every time I saw her.

"You look nice," she whispered back, her fingertips still around the stem of her glass.

"Thank you."

"You look good in a tuxedo."

"I bet it'll look better on your bedroom floor."

A slight blush entered her cheeks while a smile emerged. She covered it up by taking a drink.

"Vincent Hunt is here. Wanted to warn you."

"I saw him a few minutes ago. Has he spoken to you?"

I shook my head. "I doubt he will."

"I don't know what to expect from him."

"Don't be afraid of him."

"Who said I was?" she countered.

My eyes softened at the hardness in her voice. I couldn't wipe away the slight smile that raised the corner of my mouth. "I love you." The thought entered my brain less than a second before it left my mouth. I hadn't planned to say those words to her. They just came out unexpectedly, straight from of my heart and into her ears.

I dismissed myself from her company and ventured elsewhere. If I spent too much time at her side, it could make things suspicious. The last thing I wanted was for people to think she was a two-timing liar. People didn't understand we were in love, but I hoped one day they did.

I took my seat beside Pine at the table.

"They're supposed to serve dinner soon."

"Is that all you care about?" I asked.

"Other than women and booze, yes."

MY SPEECH WAS SHORT AND SWEET, AND I TOOK THE liberty of staring at Titan the entire time I spoke. She sat in the center of the room, so it was easy to appear to be looking at everyone. A blush entered her cheeks, a reaction she only made for me. Affection was in her eyes because she knew she was still the center of my focus—even in a room full of a thousand people.

The applause sounded, and then I took my seat.

Pine clapped me on the shoulder. "That was a great speech. Who wrote it?"

"No one."

"So you did?" he asked.

"I just made it up on the fly."

He gave me an incredulous look. "Ugh, I hate you."

The ceremony continued, and the host talked about the money we'd raised throughout the year. They opened the auction, the last push to raise as much as they could before the end of the year. Rare paintings, trips, and other donations were sold off.

I didn't buy anything.

When that was over, dinner concluded, and everyone left their seats to mingle once again.

I noticed Titan excuse herself from the circle of men she was talking to and head to the bathroom.

I wasn't going to pass up the opportunity. I'd been staring at her back all night, wanting to lavish her beautiful skin with my kisses. I wanted to taste that lipstick. I wanted to hike up her dress and fuck her up against the wall.

I excused myself and moved into the hallway, trailing

behind her. No one was around, so the opportunity was perfect. One stride equaled three of hers, making it easy to catch up to her without pushing myself.

My hand gripped her elbow, and I guided her past the bathroom and down a different hallway.

She flashed her hostile gaze at me and argued under her breath. "Hunt, no."

I pulled her around the corner and pushed her against the wall. "You don't say no to me."

"You bet your ass, I do—"

My hand circled her neck, and I kissed her. The second my lips were on hers, she was silenced. Her mouth hesitated for an instant before she kissed me back, her body succumbing to the desires we'd felt all night. I knew this couldn't last forever, not much longer than a minute or two. But I hated standing in a room with her while pretending she didn't mean the world to me. I just wanted to kiss her, to fall into the fantasy that she really was mine.

Her hands moved up my chest, and she wrapped her leg around my waist.

I pinned her against the wall and gripped her thigh while holding it around me. My chest pressed her into the wall and I kissed her, pretending her back was to my mattress and I was plowing myself deep inside her. My cock was wedged right against her clit and I ground slowly, touching her in just the right place.

She moaned into my mouth as she gripped my shoulders.

I wanted to do this forever, but minutes had already passed. If I waited too long, I was asking for trouble. I sucked her bottom lip then kissed the corner of her mouth before I pulled away, full of remorse that I had to stop.

She wore the same look of disappointment.

I hated this.

She licked her thumb then smeared it across my mouth, wiping away the lipstick stain. She kept her eyes on me as she did it, concentrating on my gaze.

I didn't give a damn about the lipstick.

She lowered her leg then cleared her throat as she smoothed out her dress.

"I'll leave first." My hand moved to hers, and I gave it a gentle squeeze before I walked away. I turned the corner, relieved not to see anyone in the hallway. And then I returned to the party, still hard in my slacks.

I was surrounded by people I knew, faces that I recognized. I'd done business with these executives, partied with some, and slept with a few others. But they were just a blur of people who really meant nothing to me. I'd shared experiences with them, but that was nothing in comparison to the experiences I had with one woman.

I didn't care about anyone there.

The only person I cared about wasn't standing beside me.

Where she belonged.

I SAW THE CROWD PART BEFORE I ACTUALLY SAW HIM.

But he was a foot taller than most people, and he had a presence that made everyone else's seem insignificant. Like a shark circling prey, he took his time getting to me, wanting my heart rate to spike just so he could listen to it in the water.

But my pulse remained exactly the same.

There wasn't a single person in the world who intimidated me.

And the one person who could get my heart rate to spike was a woman—which she did from a single look.

He approached me with the same expression of confidence. He didn't have a drink in his hand like everyone else, and one hand rested in the pocket of his slacks. His jaw was cleanly shaven, his eyes were dark, and he wore a subtly contentious expression. He stopped in front of me, facing me head on.

I met his look but didn't extend my hand.

He didn't initiate the gesture either.

Everyone was too busy with their company to notice us. Only Pine was aware of the situation because he was standing beside me. He took the cue and found something else to do.

Another minute of silence.

Hostility.

Eyes full of rage.

The standoff seemed to last forever.

He approached me, so I refused to speak first. The last thing he ever said to me was a threat—which he executed. I wasn't going to put my cards on the table when I didn't know what game we were playing. Maybe he wanted to play blackjack when I was only prepared for a round of poker.

He clenched his jaw slightly before he finally said something. "Excellent speech."

I wasn't expecting a compliment—even if it was empty. "Thank you."

"I remember when you asked me to help you on your first speech. You were running for president of your eighth-grade class." His eyes shifted back and forth as he looked into mine, absorbing every single expression I made. My face was a mask, but he searched for more anyway. "Diesel, do you remember that?"

Like it was yesterday. "Yeah. I won."

He nodded. "Yes, you did. Because I raised a winner."

His words didn't seem like a threat on the outside, but I knew everything exchanged in this conversation would be a veiled warning. I thwarted both of his plans, and he didn't swallow that well.

"I shouldn't have underestimated you."

"No, you shouldn't have."

He looked me up and down, as if he were sizing me up. "I won't make that mistake again." He prepared to walk away.

I kept my guard up, waiting for anything. He would never raise a fist to me or do something to draw attention to us both, but he was also unpredictable.

He turned back to me slightly, having one more thing to say. "Tell Titan I said hello. I'm sure you'll see her later tonight."

6
TITAN

"You don't need to walk me inside, Thorn."

He parked at the curb in his Ferrari and killed the engine. "I want to make sure you get inside alright."

"You've seen my right hook. I can knock some teeth out if I have to."

He smiled with fondness. "I know, sweetheart. But it helps me sleep better at night when I don't leave things to chance. You're the most important person in my life. I can't afford to let anything bad happen to you."

I smiled at his words, touched by his heart. Thorn didn't behave this way to the woman he bedded, at least, not to the best of my knowledge. They seemed like cold and meaningless relationships, not the kind I had with Hunt. Thorn didn't see the same woman twice, always looking for new entertainment. But when he spoke to me that way, it made me wonder if he was wasting his potential.

We got out of the car and headed into the building.

"Thorn?"

"Hmm?" He hit the button and waited for the elevator to arrive.

"You're really sweet, you know that?"

He regarded me with a confused expression. "I'm only like that to you."

"It makes me wonder if you'd be happier being sweet to someone else...someone you're in love with."

The doors opened and he stepped inside. "What are you getting at, Titan?"

I followed him inside, and the doors shut. "Are you sure you don't want to fall in love with someone? Give a relationship a chance? Because you have the potential to be a great man for the right woman."

He smirked like I'd said something funny and shrugged it off. "I'm sure."

"Have you thought about it?"

"I'm incapable of love," he said simply. "I'm sweet to you because I respect you. I'm sweet to you because I trust you. You're family to me. But everyone else out there...they mean nothing to me. I've never met a woman I've ever given a damn about. That's not how I view women. They're just objects to me. You can think less of me all you want, but that's the cold truth." He shook his head and stared at the buttons on the wall. The floor numbers lit up as we moved. "I have the perfect life. Why would I want to change it?"

I stared at his handsome face, seeing the truth in his eyes. "First of all, I don't think less of you."

He smiled again. "That's why I love you."

"I just want to make sure I'm not taking something away from you."

"Trust me, you aren't. I've never loved a woman, and I never will. And that's not because I won't allow myself to. I just don't care. One day when we're old, I won't be able to pick up women anymore. But that's fine because I'll have you. We'll love each other, have our kids, and have our success. How could I possibly want anything more than that?"

The doors opened and we stepped inside.

Hunt was sitting on the couch in the living room, a glass of scotch on the table. His bow tie was undone, and his shoes were kicked off. He must have come here straight after the charity gala, one goal on his mind.

Thorn turned to him, his carefree attitude evaporating. "Good night, Titan."

"Good night."

He stepped back into the elevator and returned to the lobby.

I set my clutch on the table and slipped my heels off.

My feet practically screamed the second they were flat again.

Hunt rose from the couch and walked toward me, his feet bare against the hardwood floor. He crowded my personal space immediately and grabbed me like he hadn't touched me in months. His hand cupped the back of my head, and he kissed me hard on the mouth, escalating our kiss the second we touched.

My hand moved to his wrist, and I kissed him back, my mouth opening with his and closing again. He gave me his tongue, and I took it greedily. I could taste champagne on his tongue, along with the distinct hint of whiskey.

His mouth broke from mine, and he trailed kisses down my jawline until he reached my neck. He buried his face in my skin and lavished me with intense kisses, his hands gripping and squeezing me.

I didn't find kissing as erotic as other things, but make-out sessions with Hunt were the biggest turn-on I'd ever had. Every time our lips moved together, I trembled. When his tongue swiped against mine, I turned to mush.

He turned me around and pressed his face directly into the back of my updo. His hands squeezed my biceps as he smelled my hair, a slight growl coming from his throat. He tilted his head down and pressed a kiss to the top of my spine. It was a wet kiss with a little tongue.

Then slowly he moved down, trailing over my bare skin until he moved to his knees on the floor. His mouth moved all the way down to the top of my ass.

I closed my eyes and moaned.

He ran his mouth all the way back to my neck then pushed the thin straps off my shoulders. The gown slid off my body until it hit the floor, revealing me standing in a black thong. I heard his clothes drop a moment later, and then his arms were wrapped around me again, his bare chest pressed against me. His chest was warm and hard, like leaning against a slab of concrete that was hot from sitting in the sun all day.

We moved to my bedroom next, and my back hit the soft sheets. Hunt pulled my thong off then positioned himself between my thighs. He didn't appear to be in charge, and I didn't want to be. Right now, we were just a man and a woman.

He folded me underneath him until I was as small as possible. He had a perfect angle, and he sank me into the mattress as he covered me like clouds covered the sun. He tilted my body then slid into me, pushing his thick cock deep inside me. It was a soft thrust, but it was packed with determination.

My arms wrapped around his neck, and my fingers dug into the back of his hair. "Diesel..." His strands were soft and thick, the same color as his dark eyes. I was stretched wide apart, stuffed with his enormous dick, and I'd never felt more like a woman. I looked into his eyes and found a connection with the dark irises that hinted of danger. He was dark, beautiful, and enormous. I widened my legs farther and pulled him harder into me, enjoying the sensation I'd been looking forward to all evening.

He moaned as his cock twitched inside me.

I'd had to stare at Hunt from across the room all night. I'd had to see his muscular shoulders in his crisp tuxedo, wishing my hands were gripping them. I had to watch him smile at his colleagues, seeing the slightest boyish charm that he possessed. I had to observe women touch him inappropriately on the arm when a hand-shake would have sufficed. I remained by Thorn's side, the exact place I belonged, and I had to pretend the love of my life wasn't standing in that same room.

I had to squeeze my thighs together as I sat because I kept picturing this moment.

One hand fisted into my hair, exactly where it belonged. He tugged on me aggressively and started to thrust, fucking me deep into my bed. His chest rubbed against my nipples as he moved, chafing them after a few strokes.

I already wanted to come. "Diesel." I'd already said his name once, but I didn't want to stop. He'd kissed me in the hallway where anyone could have seen us, but neither one of us seemed to give a damn. We just had to have each other. It didn't matter what the consequences were. "I'm so in love with you..." It was a thought that didn't come from my heart. It came from my soul. Every part of my body was hopelessly in love with this man. I was on my back with my legs spread, taking in as much of him as I could. I wanted this to last forever, to experience this beautiful high with him.

He looked into my eyes without a hint of surprise. He didn't smile or gloat, taking in the words like he'd expected to hear them all night. He continued to fuck me at the regular pace, giving it to me deep and good, but not fast and harsh. "Baby, I'm in love with you."

WE FACED EACH OTHER IN MY BED, BOTH OF US NAKED AND slightly covered by the sheets. Hunt always seemed to be warm, so the sheets only partially covered him. I usually had them pulled up to my shoulders.

His eyes were on me, etched in hardness. He stared at me like he usually did, but he seemed to be thinking of something else. It was something I'd never seen before. Ordinarily, when his eyes were on me, it meant I had his complete focus.

"What are you thinking about?"

His eyes shifted slightly as he returned to me. "The charity gala."

"Are you replaying your speech? Trust me, it was great."

He didn't crack a smile. "Not my speech."

Now I couldn't deny the annoyance on his face. "What's on your mind?"

"My father."

I'd assumed they would ignore each other like they usually did. But perhaps they'd had an interaction I didn't notice. "What happened?"

"He complimented my speech."

"That doesn't sound so bad..."

"Then he reminded me of the time he helped me prepare my speech in eighth grade. I was running for president of the student body, and he spent an entire Saturday helping me work through draft after draft until it was perfect."

I imagined a younger version of Hunt, with the same dark hair and dark eyes. Except he possessed the happiness of a young boy, someone who only cared about his friends, sports, and school crushes. "Did you win?"

"I did."

"Then it looks like you guys made a good team."

"Yeah..."

"Anything else happen?"

Hunt paused for a long time, his eyes shifting away from mine altogether. "He knows we're sleeping together."

The charming story of Hunt and his father turned into old news. "What? He said that?"

"Basically."

"But how would he know?"

He shook his head. "I don't know." He rolled to his back and stared at the ceiling. "But if anyone really pays attention, it's obvious. He probably sees the way I look at you, the way you look at me. I haven't been photographed with anyone in months. He's seen the way I bend over backward for you... It's not that surprising."

"Do you think we need to worry about it?"

He rested his hand on my chest. "He doesn't care about my personal life. He's more interested in ruining my business life. That's what matters to him."

"You're sure about that? Because that interview you gave was pretty personal."

He took a deep breath and sighed. "I don't know."

Now the terror started to seep into my chest. Vincent Hunt was a loose cannon with a need for revenge. There was no way to know what he might do.

"I know he respects you."

"Why do you say that?"

"He told me he didn't understand how I earned the love of an incredible woman like you."

My entire body softened.

"He thinks highly of you. I don't think he would do something to hurt you. You didn't do anything to him."

"I didn't take that deal."

"He knows that isn't personal."

"I took Kyle."

"He knows I'm the one who interfered with that."

Maybe there was nothing to worry about. Maybe there was.

"I think he just said that to get under my skin. I was standing in a room full of people who have no idea what's going on right under their noses. My father just wants me to know he's not stupid like everyone else."

"Maybe..." My hand moved to his chest, and I massaged his hardness.

Hunt turned silent, done with the subject.

I scooted closer to him and rested my face on his shoulder. My hair dragged across his skin, and I hooked my arm around his waist. "I don't think your father hates you."

Hunt turned his head in my direction, his lips resting against my forehead. "Then you must be confused."

"The only reason why he's doing this is because you told the public he's a terrible father."

"Because he is."

"But that's just one sliver of him. Maybe he did treat Brett badly, but your father always loved you. He spent years before that doing everything for you."

Hunt tensed visibly underneath me. "You're defending him?"

"No. Just explaining his point of view."

Hunt suddenly sat up, causing me to abruptly slide off and back onto the mattress. "Well, maybe you should stop." He faced the window, his muscular back strong and rigid.

I sat up and pulled the sheet over my chest, knowing this was tricky territory. "I think your father is just hurt and doesn't understand what to do with those emotions."

"And I think you're wrong," he said coldly.

"Why else would he bring up that story?"

"What does it matter?" He got out of bed and immediately pulled on his boxers.

"Hunt, get back in bed."

"I should get going anyway." He pulled on his slacks then grabbed his shoes. He left every night, but never this early and never angry.

"Your father never antagonized you until you went public with that story. Being estranged from you is probably difficult, but to hear you talk about him so coldly probably hurt his feelings."

"He's had years to apologize and make it right. He doesn't give a damn." He yanked his shirt on and buttoned it up. "I don't want to talk about this anymore."

I got out of bed and pulled on one of his t-shirts. "You always say you value my opinion."

"Yes." He finally turned to me, giving me a fierce stare. "About business—stuff you understand. You don't understand my father or my family. So don't bother trying." He walked around me, dismissing me coldly.

I'd never seen Hunt act this way. I'd never seen him push me away so furiously. I'd never seen him cover himself in armor and shut me out completely. "It's my job to tell you the truth, not what you want to hear. Maybe if you understand your father, you can handle him better."

"I don't want to handle him." He left the bedroom.

I followed him all the way to the elevator. "Just listen to me."

"No." He turned to face me, the loving expression long gone. "You listen to me. My father is an asshole. Always has been and always will be. He came to my office and threatened me. First, he tried to turn you against me. Then he tried to punish you for not choosing him. What kind of man does that?"

"Not once did I defend his actions."

"Didn't sound like it."

"I'm just explaining his behavior. He's not doing this because he hates you. He's doing it because you hurt him."

"What difference does it make?"

"It makes a huge difference. That means you could work it out if you wanted to."

He clenched his jaw and hit the button for the elevator. "We'll never work it out, Titan. We'll always be enemies."

"I sincerely hope not."

He shot me another glare. "I'm done talking about this."

I had more to say, but Hunt obviously didn't want to listen to it. I didn't want to push him away. The only place I wanted him was in my bed. "I didn't mean to upset you."

"Didn't seem like it." The elevator doors opened and he stepped inside.

"Please stay."

"So you can kick me out in a few hours?" He slammed his hand against the button. "No thanks." The doors closed.

I sighed and dragged my hands down my face, regretting pushing him away.

I DIDN'T CONTACT HUNT THE NEXT DAY.

He didn't talk to me either.

He didn't come by Stratosphere.

I knew he was still pissed.

Talking to him would just make him worse. I had to give him more space to come around. We hadn't fought like this since I'd gotten engaged. That had divided us, and we didn't speak for an entire week.

Now we were strangers again.

I stayed patient for the next few days. I didn't text him or bother him. He would come to me when he was ready, but I didn't want to go to him until he was ready for me.

On the fourth day, I couldn't wait any longer. I called him.

It rang for a long time. It was almost to voice mail.

He probably wouldn't answer.

Like he was waiting for the very last minute on purpose, he finally took the call. But he didn't greet me with words. He announced his presence with his silent hostility.

I could feel it like a winter chill. "Hey." I stood in my penthouse with my bare feet on the hardwood floor. I was still in my skirt and blouse because I was working at the kitchen table.

Still nothing.

"I apologized for making you upset. But I won't apologize for what I said."

Silence.

"Hunt?"

Nothing.

I wasn't going to talk to a wall. "When you're ready to talk, call me." I was about to hang up.

"Wait."

I kept the phone against my ear.

"I accept your apology. When it comes to my father... it's very difficult for me. I don't like to talk about it."

"I picked up on that."

I finally got a slight smile over the phone. It carried on into his words. "I'm sorry I was harsh."

"I accept your apology."

"I've missed you."

"Not as much as I've missed you." This was the Hunt that I liked, the affectionate but masculine version.

His smile deepened. "I'll be there in fifteen minutes."

My heart finally soared now that we were okay. The painful tension had finally passed. I knew this conversation about his father wasn't completely over. It would be revisited at some point. But for now, it was on hold. "Can you make it ten?"

7

___

HUNT

I WASN'T sure why I got so upset with Titan.

She didn't cross the line with what she said. She didn't say anything insulting.

But I didn't want to hear anything when it came to my father.

Perhaps I had more issues than I realized.

I finally returned to my office after a meeting that ran later than I anticipated. I skipped lunch because there wasn't time, and the only thing sitting in my belly was the last cup of coffee I drank.

Natalie spoke through the intercom. "Sir, Vincent Hunt is here to see you."

I froze in place, but my surprise quickly vanished. This unexpected meeting shouldn't be so unexpected. My father would execute his vendetta against me until he was finally satisfied with the results. He wanted to catch me with my pants down, see me with my guard down.

Unfortunately for him, my guard was never down.

He picked a bad time to stop by because I had more important things to worry about, but I wouldn't turn him away and look like a pussy. If I excused him, it would seem like I was avoiding him.

I didn't avoid anyone.

"Send him in," I said coldly.

"Yes, sir."

I closed my laptop, shoved my paperwork into my drawer, and hid all traces of what I was working on. I didn't want him to know more than he needed to. Mega-land could have been his, and if he knew what my plans were, it was guaranteed he would try to sabotage them.

Did other people have fathers that hated them so much?

Vincent walked inside a moment later, dressed in stealth black with a matching expression. Even his watch was black. He stared me down the second we were in the same room together. He was just as hostile as in our last encounter. He held his physique perfectly straight as he welcomed himself into my personal space. Like last time, he unbuttoned the front of his jacket before he gracefully lowered himself into the leather armchair. He crossed his legs, a black folder tucked under his arm.

This should be fun.

A long time ago, I learned to never speak first. If someone approached me, I had the upper hand. They were expected to make an explanation for their appearance. I had just to sit there and wait.

So I waited.

Nothing.

My father would drag this out as long as possible because uncomfortable silences didn't unnerve him.

They didn't unnerve me either.

His eyes remained focused on mine, the direct contact incredibly hostile. His jaw was slightly clenched, but not overly. He didn't present the folder to me, and I couldn't help but wonder what was inside.

What trick did he have up his sleeve?

Christmases had passed without a phone call. Birthdays had come and gone without a card. The anniversary of my mother's death was acknowledged in silence. I thought of him on every single important day, but I never considered contacting him. I knew he didn't consider contacting me either.

He finally pulled the folder from the crook of his arm and rested it against his knee. "This is going to be very simple."

My pulse started to escalate, knowing he was about to drop a bomb on me.

"I want Megaland. You're going to give it to me."

I tried to control my reaction, but I couldn't. My eyes constricted as they narrowed on his face. That company was mine because I made the better offer. I didn't resort to trickery to get what I wanted. I was a better businessman than he was. That was the simple truth. To demand for me to hand it over was ridiculous.

"I'm not paying you for it. Consider it a reimbursement for the private schools, college tuition, and every dime I spent raising you." He finally tossed the folder on my desk. "I want the paperwork signed this afternoon. End of story."

I didn't look at the folder because my gaze was still focused on him. I was offended by the insult, that he thought he could come in there and rob me without repercussions. I didn't negotiate with terrorists—and that was exactly what my father was. "If it's that important to you, I'll write you a check to cover every expense, from the hospital visit where I was born until the last tuition payment. But I'm not giving you that company. The guys chose me because I was the better businessman."

"They never met me, so how would they know?"

"Exactly," I countered. "I made you irrelevant, which is why I'm the better partner."

The insult must have stung, but he hid his reaction. His features were so neutral it seemed like he was sitting across from a wall rather than a person. His body remained rigid and still, the muscles of his frame keeping him perfectly straight. "Open the folder."

I held his gaze a moment longer, refusing to follow his command right away. He'd dug up something about me, but I had nothing to hide. I didn't live the life of a saint, but I never hid my visits to the underworld. I'd been seen in strip clubs, bars, on my yacht with three beautiful women all to myself. I was America's playboy, a man the media found to be a superficial heartbreaker. But they also described me as one of the most successful and intelligent business owners on the face of the planet. I didn't see how there could be anything in this folder the world hadn't already seen. My reputation was untouched because it didn't matter. As a man, I could get away with almost anything, and people didn't seem to care. If I were a woman, this would be a completely different ball game.

I pulled the folder closer to me then opened it.

It was a pile of pictures. The first one was of me kissing Titan right against the wall. We were both dressed in our finest for the charity gala that had happened last week. Her legs were hiked around my waist, and I was nearly crushing her into the wall. Even in a photograph, the heat and passion were undeniably obvious.

Fuck.

I looked at the photo underneath and saw a picture

of myself entering Titan's building at eleven in the evening. There was another of me kissing her in the office at Stratosphere. It was taken from the Chrysler building across the street. My father must have positioned people all over the place in the hopes of getting a shot the second we let our guards down.

Jesus Christ.

I didn't look any further because I'd seen enough. My eyes rose to his face, and I held his expression, still wearing my poker face. I had very low expectations of my father, but this, by far, had exceeded them.

Asshole.

The second I knew my father was onto us, we should have been smarter about it. We should have taken precautions to make sure we weren't seen. I was normally a careful man, but my intense love blinded my ability to think clearly.

Now I was paying the price for it.

A slight smile came across his face, which was filled with a gentle gloat. "Give me Megaland, or I'll hand these over to every major publication. Titan will be seen as a two-timing whore, and her empire will fall. She'll lose her endorsements, her reputation, and worst of all, her respect."

I'd never wanted to hit my father more than I did at that moment. "She's not a whore."

"Never said she was. But that's how the world will see her."

"She's not a cheater either. She and Thorn—"

"Don't care. Give me Megaland, Diesel."

I didn't want to cave to a man so evil in nature. He was exploiting the love of my life to get what he wanted. It was dirty and not respectable. The cruelty was horrific, and I felt helpless to do anything about it. I'd invested a lot of time and money into that company. It was on track to be one of the biggest electronic brands in the world. Now it was being ripped out of my hands, and I couldn't do anything to stop it. "I thought you liked Titan." It was one thing to manipulate me because, in a way, I deserved it. But to bring someone else into our drama was just spiteful.

"I'm very fond of her."

"Then why would you do this to her?"

"It's just business," he said simply. "Nothing personal."

"Nothing personal?" I asked incredulously. "You're threatening to ruin everything she built just to screw me over."

"That's how the world works."

"For an asshole like you, maybe," I snapped. "Leave her out of it." I slid the folder back across the desk. "You have beef with me, not her. She's a good person and doesn't deserve this."

"Couldn't agree more." He rested his arms on the armrests of his chair, making himself comfortable in his enemy's lair. "She's got ruthless intelligence, extreme poise, and she not only keeps up with the men, but she beats them at their own game. I completely understand your fascination with her. She's exceptional."

"Then back off." I kept my voice steady, but my tone deepened with anger.

A soft smile spread across his face. "Give me what I want, and I will."

I clenched my jaw, so angry I couldn't even think straight.

My father continued to smile because he knew he had me. "We both already know how this is going to end. You're just drawing it out and making it more painful."

"What makes you think I'll agree?" He had pictures of us together, but he didn't know anything about our relationship. He didn't know what it was like when it was just the two of us. He couldn't wrap his mind around the kind of love we had—because he'd never experienced it. He was an empty vessel without a soul.

He released a faint chuckle. "Diesel, let's not play games. I know you're stupidly in love with this woman—and she's just as in love with you. She'd do anything for you, and I have no doubt you'll give me whatever I want to protect her."

God fucking dammit.

"You want to know how I know?"

I kept my silence.

"You look at her the way I used to look at your mother."

For a millisecond, the rage disappeared. Time stood still, and I remembered seeing my parents together in the living room after I was supposed to be in bed. They would sit together at the end of the couch, their bodies wrapped around each other as they enjoyed a bottle of wine. There was lots of touching, kissing, and laughter. The TV wasn't on, and only the fire burned in the fireplace. My father used to smile a lot. After she was gone, I never saw him smile like that again.

My father rose to his feet and left the folder on the desk. "My team will be in touch. I expect to sign those papers this afternoon."

I didn't object, seething in my silence. Megaland was one of my greatest achievements, and I had to hand it over without a fight. I had to submit to this man's cruelty and behave like a puppet. It went against everything I believed in, but I couldn't let him ruin Titan. It wasn't an idle threat, and I knew he would make good on his word. The world would turn against Titan, crucifying her for being a liar, a cheater, and a whore. It would hurt Thorn too, which would break Titan's heart.

I couldn't let that happen to her.

Not to the woman I loved.

He buttoned the front of his suit and headed to the door. "I'll see you soon, Diesel." He shut the door then was gone.

That's when I finally lost my shit and threw everything off the desk, breaking my laptop, slamming my phone against the wall, and scattering everything I'd been working on onto the floor. The pictures of Titan and me escaped from the folder and landed on top of the mess, as if they were purposely haunting me.

Fuck.

WITH OUR LEGAL TEAMS AND THE CONSENT OF THE OTHER three owners, we signed the paperwork in one of my conference rooms.

I signed every line, initialed when required, and gave one of my biggest accomplishments to my greatest enemy.

I handed everything across the table, and his team looked it over.

Vincent only had eyes for me, enjoying every second of his victory. He couldn't hide his silent gloat, his satisfying revenge. I'd publicly humiliated him, and now he was doing the same to me. The world wouldn't know about the new ownership of Megaland right away, but eventually, the news would travel.

When everything was completed to their satisfaction, the meeting was adjourned.

The company was no longer mine.

I lost five million dollars in one day. The money didn't bother me, but the forced default was humiliating.

But I wouldn't have it any other way. Money was just money. Titan's reputation was priceless.

The team walked out, but my father remained behind. Probably to get in the last word before he walked off with the company I had won fair and square.

But I walked up to him and faced him with the same squared shoulders and straight spine. I held my head high and refused to acknowledge this as a defeat. He'd lost my mother and two of his sons, so now all he had was money. But I had something far more valuable. I had the love of an amazing woman—and I loved her even more. That was worth more than all my assets combined.

Everyone left the room, so Vincent stared at me, eye level with me because we were the exact same height. "You love her. She loves you. So why is she marrying Thorn?"

I didn't know what his question meant. On the surface, it seemed genuine, like a father asking his son if everything was okay. There was no benefit to knowing this information. All he should care about was having dirt on me. But perhaps I was overthinking it. "It's complicated."

His eyes shifted back and forth as he looked into my gaze. The same deep brown eyes stared back at me, the same ones I'd been staring at all my life. They looked exactly the same whether he was angry or calm. "If you want her, then make it uncomplicated."

I SAT ON THE COUCH IN MY LIVING ROOM WITH A COLD BEER in front of me. I still wore my suit, but I undid my tie the second I walked inside. It was one of those nights when I needed something more than a beer, something stronger to accompany my misery. So I grabbed a cigar and smoked it right in the living room even though it would smell for a few days.

I didn't give a damn.

I debated telling Titan everything that happened. She would be sympathetic and give me the kind of affection to chase away the pain. But if I'd told her the truth, she would have told me not to take the deal.

Knowing her, she would rather take the fall than let me suffer.

She would march down to my father's office and give him a piece of her mind.

So it was best if I didn't say anything.

She'd feel terrible if she knew what I sacrificed for her.

She might find out some other way, but by then, enough time would have passed that I would be over it. And if she knew my father had pictures of us together, she would get paranoid. She might stop sleeping with me altogether.

I'd stay quiet.

Normally, I'd already be at her place with my clothes on her bedroom floor. My sorrow and desire would be buried between her legs at this very moment. We'd be completely connected, mind, body, and soul. She'd tell me she loved me just before she came, and I'd say it back while edging myself.

But I wasn't in the mood to do anything tonight other than smoke my cigar.

I wished my mother were still alive. Life would be so much different. My father would still be happy, Brett would have had the same childhood I did, and I wouldn't have one of the biggest suits in the world as my enemy. My mother was the glue that kept us all together. But now that she was no longer around, we moved further apart from each other.

She'd be disappointed in all of us.

Especially me.

My phone sat on the coffee table and lit up with a message from Titan. *Miss you.*

I stared at the message and took another puff of my cigar. The words went straight down to my crotch, making me hard. When I read the words, I could hear her sexy voice. I could hear the slight desperation in the way she spoke.

I wanted to avoid her because I wouldn't be able to fake a different mood. I was livid with my father, and nothing would change that, not even good sex. But I wanted to get lost in her embrace, to make love and forget all the bullshit surrounding our lives. Only Titan could sheathe my anger, could make me smile in the midst of grief.

I wasn't just angry that I'd lost Megaland.

I was devastated my own father would blackmail me like that.

My own flesh and blood.

Why hadn't my mother lived and my father died?

Did it make me evil for even thinking that?

Her message went unanswered for thirty minutes. I wanted to say something back, but I was too overwhelmed with my self-destructive thoughts to do anything but smoke. I smoked my cigar until I reached the butt then dropped it into the ashtray.

I wrote back. *I always miss you.*

Good. Because I just stepped inside the lobby of your building.

She wanted me badly. She didn't wait for me to come

to her. I loved that about her. If she wanted something, she made it happen.

She didn't waste time.

The elevator beeped before the doors opened. She stepped inside with her beautiful legs in stilettos. She wore a long black jacket to protect her from the cold. She stepped inside, her long brown hair straight and shiny. The jacket was instantly removed, and she made herself at home.

I walked toward her and dropped my jacket as I went.

The second she looked at me, her face hardened as she recognized the unease in my expression. She knew me well enough to understand if I was being haunted by demons she couldn't see. Her hand moved to my chest, and she parted her lips to speak.

"I don't want to talk about it." My hand slid into her hair as I prepared to kiss her. "But I want you to make me forget about it." My mouth moved to hers and we combined our lips. I felt her bottom lip and sucked it gently before I gave her my tongue. My hand tugged on her hair gently, and I deepened our kiss, immediately finding comfort in our heated touch.

She undressed me with confident fingers, peeling my clothes away until I was naked. Her fingers explored the hard lines of my body, feeling my impeccable chest and tight abs. She loved my shoulders the best, so she visited those frequently.

I loved the dresses she wore because they were so easy to remove. Once the zipper was down, it fell away. Her bra and panties came next, and then this gorgeous woman was in just heels.

I kept the shoes on.

I lifted her into the air and carried her into my bedroom. I wanted her on her back, knees spread, and my entire cock buried inside her. I wanted it deep and slow, coming in her over and over again.

I wanted to come until she couldn't take any more.

I got her on the mattress, her head placed perfectly on a pillow, and then I slid inside her with one heavy thrust.

Her mouth fell open, and she gripped my biceps as she felt my large length press inside her.

My arms pinned her knees back, and I folded her underneath me. I pressed her into the mattress, made her sink deep into the bed, and then I moved. I moved hard and fast, getting up to speed right from the beginning. My cock enjoyed her wet tightness, and I quickly fell into the passion that blocked out the rest of the world.

I wanted to do this every night.

I wanted to fuck her the second I came home from work every day.

My cock only wanted this perfect pussy.

"Baby..." A deep moan erupted from the back of my

throat. When I slid through her perfection, I didn't care about the nightmares that lived outside the four walls of my penthouse. The connection between us was powerful enough to make me forget my hardships and heartbreaks. The loss of my company seemed insignificant when I had something so much better.

I just wished she were truly mine.

Her nipples hardened, and she began to hold her breath, preparing for the wonderful explosion between her legs. "I love you." She fisted my short hair and gripped my shoulder, another wave of moisture erupting between her legs. She said those words to me more often now than she did before.

I'd fallen in love with her more with every passing day, so it didn't surprise me. Hearing her confession of love always made me feel more like a man. It comforted me because I knew we would be okay. Our love was strong enough to protect us. It would bring us together eventually. I wasn't scared about her ending up with Thorn.

I knew she'd end up with me.

Eventually. "I love you too, baby."

8

TITAN

THORN and I got dinner together at a new restaurant that had just opened. The chef was from France, and he cooked up the most exquisite delicacies. It was French, infused with American favorites.

We sat across from each other and shared a bottle of wine. I'd cut down my whiskey intake to a single glass a day. I replaced my old habit with water, iced tea, and wine. My palate was different now that my taste buds weren't soaked in whiskey. It was slightly refreshing, although I missed drinking the way I used to.

"What's new with you?" Thorn wore black slacks and a black collared shirt, the top button undone. His tanned skin was visible, along with the prominent cords in his neck. He ran through Central Park in the afternoons, and that's where he got his skin exposure. The room was full of couples and beautiful women at the bar, but as Thorn vowed, he didn't pay attention to anyone else but me.

It was nice.

I would never be the recipient of romantic affection, but he certainly made me feel loved. And he would make me feel like a treasured wife.

The second I thought of our wedding, I thought of Hunt.

It was impossible not to.

The second I became Thorn's wife, I knew our relationship would be over. That might be why I'd become more passionate with him recently, telling him I loved him because I knew I wouldn't always have the opportunity. One day, he would have a new woman on his arm as we passed each other at a common function. It would hurt to look at him, but at least I would know I told him how I felt when I had the chance.

Before a different woman replaced me in his bed.

Sometimes it scared me how much I loved that man when I didn't trust him. How could I be so infatuated with someone when I was so uneasy? It didn't make sense to me. The behavior was out of character for me.

Thorn cocked his head to the side. "Titan?"

"Hmm?" My eyes shifted back to him, and I took a drink.

"I asked what's new with you?"

I heard him but didn't properly digest the words. "Nothing. What about you?"

"Everything alright?" he asked, his gaze protective.

"I was just thinking about work..."

"Be more specific."

I spoke the first thing that came to mind. "Sales at Stratosphere have been incredible. Much higher than Hunt and I anticipated. We're pleased with the results."

"Because the two of you are geniuses." He tapped his temple with his forefinger. "And geniuses make great things happen."

"You're too kind," I said with a smile.

"I'm not a fan of his, but I admire the way he makes money. Knows what he's doing."

"Very true." I'd seen Hunt in action, seen the way his mind worked a million miles an hour. He could construct an original plan with the same tools as everyone else, but his indirect marketing approaches had much greater effect. In addition to that, the respect he'd built in the business world always helped out in our favor. He could make things happen far quicker than I because people were always anxious to work with him.

Anything Hunt touched turned to gold.

"My assistant got in contact with that wedding planner from Martha's Vineyard. They said they have an opening in February. What do you say?"

That was eighteen months away. It seemed like a

longer engagement than we'd originally agreed upon. "That's a long engagement, but that's okay with me."

"No, this February," he corrected. "So in a few months."

I held my glass but didn't take a drink. "Oh...I'm surprised they even have an opening."

"They moved some stuff around, I guess," Thorn said.

"Could we even pull a wedding off that quickly?"

"She'll handle the decorations, food, beverages, all that stuff. I know you don't want to do that anyway. All you need to worry about is getting your dress. So time shouldn't be an issue."

I should be thrilled by that news, but I was only filled with dread. I thought I would have more time to enjoy Hunt, but if I was getting married in three months, our relationship would end much sooner than I anticipated.

Thorn drank from his glass and watched my expression. "Is that alright?"

"Yeah...it's just sudden."

His gaze became more intrusive as he began to analyze my unhappy expression. "We don't have to do it that soon. We can do it whenever you want. I just thought we wanted to get it done as quickly as possible."

"I guess I was expecting a longer engagement than that."

"How long?" he asked.

"A year or so."

"But we don't really need a long engagement. Neither one of us is planning this, so the extra time doesn't seem relevant. But you're the bride, so whatever you want." Thorn didn't pressure me, but I knew he was disappointed.

I could drag it out longer, but I knew it wouldn't make much of a difference. My relationship with Hunt was doomed to die anyway. The longer I let it continue, the harder it would be to end. "February is fine."

"You're sure?" he asked. "Because we don't even have to do it at Martha's Vineyard if you want."

"It'll be beautiful there, especially in the winter."

"Then I'm going to tell Angela to book it."

"Alright."

"Perfect. Looks like we have a date."

"What's the date?" I asked.

"February twelfth."

I took a long drink, downing the entire contents of the glass before I refilled it. "The twelfth it is."

I WAS DOING REALLY WELL UNTIL I RELAPSED.

I drank more in one sitting than I ever had in my life. I made my favorite drink over and over, drowning myself in the whiskey that I adored so much. Picking a wedding date screwed me up in the head.

It dragged me down into the depths.

It suffocated me.

This was what I wanted. This was the path I chose.

But it brought me so much heartache.

Even if I wanted to change my mind, I couldn't. I'd already made a commitment to Thorn, and I couldn't back out now. It would be a betrayal to our friendship. It would make him look like a fool to the entire world.

No, I'd never do that to him.

I'd always been a regular drinker, but I'd never lost control of my faculties. I'd never even been drunk.

I just drank a lot. Big difference.

But now I seemed to be making up for all the liquor I'd skipped. Now I was plumping my cells with the alcohol they craved. It soothed my emotions and slowly numbed me so I didn't have to deal with reality.

It was easier to cope that way.

I WOUND UP IN THE ELEVATOR OF HUNT'S BUILDING, MY body weaker than usual because I'd drunk too much. I didn't consider myself drunk, but I was definitely slightly impaired. Thankfully, I had a driver, so I never had to worry about getting myself anywhere.

The doors opened to his living room, and I stepped inside.

Hunt was in the kitchen, the sound of dishes moving and the water running reaching my ears. Everything stopped when he heard me, and he emerged a moment later in just his sweatpants.

The way I was hoping he would be dressed.

A prominent V was chiseled into his waistline, extending up his hips and framing the eight-pack he displayed. The muscles of his abdomen shifted as he walked toward me. His pecs remained as a solitary wall, unflinching as he approached me.

Wordlessly, his arms moved around my waist, and he leaned in and kissed me.

I kissed him back, falling into the addiction that brought me the most joy. Whiskey used to be my drug, but it had a nasty bite if I took too much. With Hunt, I could never get enough.

His sultry kiss died away, and he leaned back to look at me. His gaze moved to my lips, but not in the intense way I was used to. It was full of suspicion, and then a moment later, disappointment. "You've been drinking."

"Yeah..."

"A lot."

My hands remained on his biceps, my fingertips digging into his muscles. He was warm, smooth, and hard all at the same time.

His look of disappointment didn't change. He stared at me fiercely, as if he wanted to berate me but couldn't find the right words.

"It won't happen again...I was doing well. I just had a slipup."

His hands squeezed my hips slightly before he removed the pressure. "Promise me, baby?"

My eyes felt lidded and heavy, and while I was tired, I was also more affectionate. I wanted his hot lips all over me. "I promise."

That seemed to be enough for him because he kissed me on the forehead, forgiving me for my stupid mistake. "What happened?" His lips moved against my forehead as he spoke.

"I don't want to talk about it..." If I told him I was depressed about the wedding, he would attempt to talk me out of it. It would lead to a painful conversation I couldn't have again. It would just give him hope that there would be a different outcome for us. I didn't want to torture him or myself.

His hand moved to my cheek, and he lifted my gaze, forcing me to look at him. "Tell me."

I looked into his powerful eyes and suddenly felt helpless. When it came to this masculine man, with his corded forearms, his chiseled jaw, and striking resemblance to danger, I wanted to drop all my armor and expose myself to him entirely—even if he hurt me.

"Thorn and I set a date, and it's a lot sooner than I thought it would be..."

He didn't react. "When?"

"February twelfth."

His hand remained on my cheek, and he looked at me with the same expression. He must have thought I was drunk because he didn't try to make an argument like he normally would. All he did was listen.

"I'm not ready to let you go... I'm ridiculously in love with you." Damn, maybe I was drunk. I blurted out everything like a damn idiot. I'd said I loved him before in the heat of the moment, and that was pretty much the same thing as being drunk. "I don't want to see you with someone else... I get so jealous. I don't want to lose what we have because it's so damn good...but I have to let you go."

"No, you don't," he whispered.

"Yes, I do..."

"Well, I'll never let you go." He lifted me into his arms and carried me into the bedroom. Clothes came off, and our naked bodies wrapped around each other. He was inside me instantly, my back to the mattress as I sank toward the earth. My ankles locked around his waist and we moved hard together, getting as much of each other as we could. We screwed like this was the last night we would ever be together.

"Please don't."

WHEN I WOKE UP THE NEXT MORNING, I HAD A MASSIVE migraine.

Maybe I did drink too much.

I'd never drunk like that in my entire life—besides my father's funeral. Getting drunk was the only way I could stop myself from crying.

My hand moved to Hunt beside me, but he was nowhere to be found. The sheets were still warm like he'd been there recently. It was the first time we'd spent the night together in months, and I'd slept like a rock through the night.

But that also could have been because I blacked out.

I opened his nightstand, hoping there would be a bottle of painkillers inside. I reached my hand in and came into contact with a hard book. I leaned over and squinted, trying to read even though my eyes hadn't adjusted to being open just yet. After I pulled it to my face, I recognized it.

My father's book.

My hands slightly shook as I felt it. There was a bookmark in the pages, toward the very end. It was a receipt. I opened to the right page and looked at the date. It showed he'd bought the book months ago.

Before we called things off.

I could only assume he'd been reading it. Why else

would he buy it? But why hadn't he told me he'd been reading it? I had so many questions, but it didn't seem appropriate to ask him. It looked like I was going through his personal belongings when that wasn't my intention. I flipped through the pages and found little marks with a pen. Some passages were underlined, perhaps one that he enjoyed.

I panicked when I heard footsteps coming from the bathroom, so I placed the book back in the drawer and quickly shut it. The pulse was throbbing in my temple, but I lay back and pretended to have been there the entire time.

He entered the bedroom with a towel around his waist. "Morning, baby."

"Morning." Once I looked at his perfect, naked body, I stopped thinking about the book. Little drops dripped down the grooves of his gorgeous chest. My tongue wanted to taste him everywhere. My migraine was forgotten.

"How are you feeling?" He leaned over me on the bed and ran his fingers through my hair.

It dulled the pain, temporarily. "I've been better."

A handsome smile spread across his mouth. "First time I've ever seen you drunk."

"I wasn't drunk."

"I bet you don't remember most of the things you said last night."

I remembered talking in front of the elevator, but most of it was blurry.

He grinned in arrogance.

"What did I say...?"

He kissed the corner of my lips. "You'll never know." He moved off me and dropped the towel from around his waist. He stood at the dresser and pulled out a pair of boxers, his tight ass looking unbelievable.

I nearly drooled.

"Want some breakfast?"

"I should probably get going..."

"Nope." He turned around and came back toward me on the bed. "Breakfast and then sex."

"You don't have work?"

"I always have work. But business will carry on even if I'm not there. Come on."

"I'll stay under one condition."

"Name it." He held himself on top of me again, smelling like fresh body soap and cologne.

"I need some painkillers for my migraine. And you do the cooking."

He grinned. "I can do that."

THORN AND I TALKED ABOUT BUSINESS IN MY OFFICE, about what we would do with our respective companies once they were combined. We held assets in very different fields, and if we combined them correctly, we could achieve great success.

But Hunt was on my mind again.

He'd been in my head more than usual that week. I kept thinking about my father's book sitting in his night-stand. It was a mystery why he never mentioned it to me. Knowing he read my father's work, essentially, his diary, meant more to me than I could put into words. I never asked him to read it. He did that entirely on his own.

Every time I was with Thorn, I thought about the wedding. And the more I thought about it, the more uneasy I became. I was so certain this was the right choice for me, but now it didn't seem that way. My doubt had nothing to do with Thorn, who was one of the greatest men I'd ever known.

It only had to do with Hunt.

Thorn finished what he was saying then set the paperwork on my desk. "So you still aren't going to change your name?"

My entire identity was based on my last name. It was the name my father gave to me. The moment I changed it, the name would be lost forever. If I didn't pass it on to my children, it would cease to exist. It wouldn't even make sense for people to refer to me as Titan anymore. And I certainly wouldn't allow anyone to address me as Tatum. "No."

He rolled his eyes. "Meet me halfway. Let's do a hyphen, at least."

"No."

His look hardened.

"My name is important to me, Thorn. How would you feel if I asked you to change your name?"

"I get where you're coming from, but—"

"It's totally sexist."

"It's tradition."

"Whatever," I said. "My father gave me that name. It means a lot to me."

"And I get that. Which is why I suggested a hyphen. Titan can go first if you want. Titan-Cutler."

Even that didn't feel right to me. "I'm sorry."

"You won't have the same last name as your children. You do realize that, right?"

"They'll have hyphened names."

He rubbed his temple as he sighed in irritation. "We aren't doing that."

"You bet your ass, we are. Titan is everything that I am. I can't change my identity for someone else, Thorn. I'm sorry. It would be different if we were in love, but we aren't. This is a business relationship as well as one for convenience. I won't change my mind about this." When Hunt and I discussed it, I had a more open attitude about it—but it was because I was desperately in love with him. This situation was totally different.

Thorn shook his head slightly but folded. "I accept your decision. But I think we'll need to revisit it once we have our first child."

It wouldn't go any differently then. "Fine."

Thorn continued to sit in the armchair even though it was tense between us. It didn't constitute a fight, but it wasn't easy either. Normally, things between us were absolutely smooth. Since we were making big decisions, there were bumps and potholes in the way. He watched me for a few minutes before he changed the subject. "Anything else we need to discuss before I leave? I'll be in Montreal for a few days."

"When will you be back?"

"Friday. It's a short trip."

"It'll be beautiful. I'm sure it's snowing."

"I'm looking forward to it. Perhaps I can find someone to share my chalet with."

I smiled. "With your charm, I'm sure you will."

"Thank you. I'm looking forward to you being the recipient of that charm."

I found Thorn attractive, but I didn't see him in that way. Before I met Hunt, I could picture us having a great sex life. He was beautiful, muscular, successful...everything I wanted in a partner. But the moment I fell in love, my physical attraction to other men disappeared. Now I couldn't even imagine it. "I slept over at Hunt's place the other night..."

Thorn shifted his position in the chair as he watched me.

"I had a migraine, so I opened his nightstand drawer and found my father's book..."

"His book of poetry?" he asked in surprise.

"Yeah. He had a bookmark in it along with some notes, so he seems to be reading it."

Thorn rubbed his chin as he considered me. "What's your point?"

"I checked the receipt, and he bought it before we broke up."

Thorn stared at me.

"I don't know why I'm telling you this. I'm just not sure what to make of it."

"Maybe he enjoys poetry. I read sometimes."

"Yeah, but he's never mentioned it to me. Not once."

"I still don't see the relevance."

"It's just...it's a very sweet thing to do. I don't see why he would do that if he didn't really love me. If he was just using me before we broke up, it doesn't make sense for him to buy my father's book and read it."

Thorn considered me for a long time. He didn't seem annoyed by my words, but he needed to take time to phrase a response. "I think you might be reading too much into it."

"What do you mean?"

"He may have bought that book to learn more about

you, to make you fall in love with him to achieve his goals. Or maybe he really did buy it because he wanted to read your father's work. Maybe he bought a used copy and never read it. The fact that he never mentioned it to you makes it seem like he doesn't want you to know."

I hadn't considered any of those other scenarios. I just assumed it was a touching and romantic gesture.

"I'm not trying to disappoint you," he said gently. "I just see these flashes of hope in your eyes. They come and go over and over. It's painful to watch..."

I shifted my eyes away, embarrassed I was so obvious.

"I know this is hard for you," he continued. "I know the wedding date reminds you that you and Hunt will be over soon, and that scares you. I get it. You think you've unmasked something to make him innocent and you can finally have everything that you want. But you need to understand that's never coming. If Hunt could clear himself, he would have done it by now. You're in the exact position you were in months ago, but your emotions cloud your judgment over and over. I'm not saying this in judgment. I'm just trying to give you a clear perspective on the situation."

Thorn understood me too well. My eyes remained on the desk because I didn't have the strength to look at him. "You're right... I guess I'll never stop hoping. It's hard for me to stay objective when it comes to him. It's impossible...and I start to fantasize."

"It's okay," he whispered. "That's what I'm here for. You can always talk to me about these things."

"I know you're tired of hearing them..."

"Not true."

I raised my expression to meet his gaze.

"You can talk to me about anything, Titan. I will always be there for you—even if you repeat it a million times. I'm your partner for life, whether I'm your husband or not. There's never something you can't share with me. I hate seeing you in pain like this. I wish more than you that it had worked out with Hunt. I'll never forget how ecstatic you were when you told me you were going to marry him. I've never seen you so full of joy like that since the day I met you...but I have to protect you too. I can't tell you what you want to hear to make you happy. I have to give you the truth—as painful as it is to listen to."

My eyes softened as I listened to Thorn be sweet to me—for the millionth time. "I know..."

"I've talked you back down to earth today, but in a few weeks, we'll be back where we are right now. But don't worry, I'll be there for you again...just like you would be for me."

"Thank you."

"No problem, sweetheart."

"I don't know what it is about him that makes me like this..."

"It's love," he said simply. "It's the strongest emotion in the world. It was love that made me stab someone in the heart to protect you. It was the craziest thing I've ever done. I could have gone to jail for murder, but I didn't care. And I'd do it a million times just to keep you safe. So I understand, Titan. I've never been in love, and I can imagine that level of love is a million times more blinding."

9

HUNT

I DIDN'T READ up on Megaland because I didn't want to know what my father was doing with my company.

I mean, *his company.*

There wasn't a doubt in my mind he would take care of the company, but I was disappointed he saw what direction I was taking it in. It was basically like looking at my playbook.

It was unfortunate.

Even as weeks went by, I couldn't swallow the defeat. He came into my office and robbed me, but I did nothing to stop it. All I could do was put my hands in the air and let him walk out—with my balls in his pocket.

I sacrificed business for romance.

Something I promised myself I would never do.

But Titan was my woman, and I loved her too damn

much to let anything bad happen to her. She worked so hard to retain respect from men in her field. If the world thought she was cheating on Thorn with me, she would never live it down. It would haunt her for decades.

My company wasn't worth that lifetime of sorrow.

Besides, she was going to be my wife someday.

I didn't know how, but she would. She'd arrived at my penthouse drunk and said everything I wanted to hear. She had doubts about her marriage to Thorn. She wanted to marry me instead. Liters of alcohol showed her true colors, her profound vulnerability. She was just as weak as I was, miserable at the thought of letting me go.

We would make this work.

I needed to do something to make her choose me, but I didn't know what else I could do. I had no evidence to support my innocence. All I could do was show her how much I loved her with every action I took.

Eventually, the lack of evidence wouldn't matter.

She simply couldn't live without me.

The way I couldn't live without her.

I was at my office when the news showed a video that had been released to the press—and it included me.

Someone had sent in a video of my father and me from the charity gala. We spoke to each other in the corner of the room, both of us fiercely hostile with unnecessary space in between us. There was no audio, thankfully. But it was obvious we hated each other. We didn't even shake hands.

The story accompanying the video made it even worse.

Vincent and Diesel Hunt are still at war with one another, over a decade into their feud. A few months ago, Diesel Hunt shared his version of the story with one of our team members, and this evidence seems to support his account. Vincent Hunt is seen standing across from his own son and doesn't even offer a handshake. Few words are exchanged before he abruptly walks away. Did Vincent Hunt treat his son just as badly as his stepson, Brett Maxwell? We reached out to Vincent Hunt's office for comment but haven't received a response.

"Jesus Christ..." I rubbed my temple as I listened to the rest of the story, which made my father sound like an even bigger scumbag. Technically, it was completely accurate, but I didn't need any more fuel added to the fire. He already took Megaland away from me. I didn't want to make my life even more difficult.

But he wouldn't take this lying down. My father was stubborn and prideful. He didn't care much about what other people thought of him, but having the entire world critique his parenting skills would unnerve him.

It was only a matter of time before I heard from him again.

My cell phone rang, and I saw Titan's name on the

screen. She never called me during business hours, so I knew exactly what this was about. I answered. "Hey, baby." I didn't think twice before I spoke to her that way. No one was in my office, so I could say whatever the hell I wanted. Besides, I wasn't in the mood to censor myself.

She didn't correct me, which told me she knew about the news story. "I'm assuming you already saw it."

"Yep, just finished," I said with a sigh.

"I wonder who got that video."

"Don't know. Don't care." In a world of social media and endless cameras, it was impossible for every little detail not to be captured.

"He's not going to like this, is he?"

"Nope." He'd probably already punched a hole in the wall by now.

"Maybe you should be proactive and tell him you had nothing to do with this."

I wasn't doing a damn thing, not when he came down here and threatened to destroy my woman's life. "No."

"Diesel—"

"No." I wasn't telling her what I did, not yet. And I definitely wasn't going to tell her over the phone. "It is what it is. He's a smart man. I'm sure he'll figure out I had nothing to do with this."

"But you did indirectly cause it."

There was no denying that.

"Do you need anything?" she asked quietly. She

took time out of her busy day just to call me. I knew very few people were afforded that luxury, earned her devoted concern. As far as I knew, it was just Thorn and me.

"No."

Titan knew my bad attitude wasn't going to change. "Alright. I'll talk to you later."

I shouldn't be a dick to her, not when she was just checking on me. She didn't deserve that. So I forced myself to speak, even through gritted teeth. "Thank you for calling me."

"You don't need to thank me, Diesel. Bye."

In a moment of weakness, I did something I'd never done before. "Love you." I'd heard tons of people say it to their significant others over the phone, but I'd never done it before. The words shot out like they had their own power. It didn't matter how angry I was, I should always show her what she meant to me. I lost my temper once before and pushed her away unnecessarily. It was a dick move. Now that I could lose her at any moment, I had to fight even harder for her.

"Love you too."

AN HOUR BEFORE THE OFFICE CLOSED, NATALIE SPOKE through the intercom. "Sir...Vincent Hunt is here to see you." Her voice shook in a way it never had before. It even cracked a little, like the pressure was too much.

I suspected my father hadn't said a word to her. He probably walked inside and just stared at her, knowing she would figure out exactly what he wanted.

It's what I would do. "Send him in, Natalie." This time, I was prepared for this arrival. This time, I knew what was coming. He'd stopped by my office unexpectedly in the past, but now I always expected him, every minute of the day.

He stepped inside my office, a powerhouse in a navy blue suit. With a different watch on his wrist and shiny shoes on his feet, he moved at a quick pace, his massive shoulders rigid with his intense rage.

I could feel it.

He dropped into the chair and set his fierce expression on me. It was different from all the others because this was a new level of anger. If the desk weren't in between us, he might throw a punch right into my jaw.

I held his gaze without blinking.

He didn't drag out the tension like he usually did. This time, he got right to the point. "Bridges continue to burn, but you never learn."

"It wasn't me."

His eyes narrowed in hostility, and he didn't show an ounce of belief. "I taught you to be a man. And men don't lie. Whatever your crime may be, you fess up to it. You do your time and walk away free."

"I know." I leaned back in my chair. "And I still didn't do it. Someone else must have leaked that to the press and got a nice paycheck out of it."

My father stared at me with increased anger. This conversation seemed to be making him more upset, not less. "I'm sick of your bullshit, Diesel. You went to the world and painted me as the bad guy. But they don't understand what you took away from me."

"I didn't take anything away from you."

He rose to his feet and stood over my desk, casting a shadow like a tall mountain. "You took away the most important thing in the world. And now I'm going to take away the most important thing in the world to you."

Titan. "You already took Megaland. Give it a rest."

He gripped the edge of my desk, his veins expanding with the tension. His jaw was so tight it might snap in half. His eyes remained the same, but they always looked full of rage anyway. "End things with Titan. Or I'm sending every photograph to the press."

This was worse than taking Megaland. This was the worst thing he could possibly do to me. He could wipe my bank accounts clean, but I would still be fine. But to take away the one thing that made me happy was insufferable. I rose to my feet and met his gaze. "Keep her out of this. This is between you and me."

"You were the one who got her involved in the first place, Diesel. You threw me under the bus to spare her."

I still didn't know how he knew that. My father was unnaturally intelligent. He'd skipped several grades in school when he was young, and he graduated at the top of his class from Harvard. He was the smartest man I knew, but this still surprised me. "It doesn't make the story untrue."

"But you didn't have to tell the world about our dirty laundry. You crossed a line."

"And you crossed a line when you threw Brett out on his ass."

"He was an adult. It was time he grew up anyway."

I knew he would never see Brett as one of us. They had no genetic relation, but that shouldn't change anything. "Leave Titan out of this. I mean it. I've given you Megaland. You've already won, alright? You beat me. Congratu-fucking-lations."

His eyes narrowed. "You think we're even?"

"More than even."

"You destroyed my reputation. You told the world only one side of the story, and I've never had the chance to say mine. Now they think I'm some heartless father who doesn't give a damn about his family."

"And is that untrue?" I snapped. "It's dead on. We haven't spoken once in the last ten years. I've gone to mom's grave every single year, and I've never seen you there—not once."

He stood back, his arms shaking with anger. It was unclear what would happen next because it seemed like he might actually hit me. "Because her grave is in my heart." He jabbed his finger into his chest as he spoke. "Because every damn day it's her funeral again. It's her birthday again. It's our wedding again. Don't stand there and act like I don't love your mother just as much now as I did when she was alive."

I'd never heard him say anything about her since she'd died. He was dead silent about it. After her funeral, he became a different person. He never mentioned her.

"Don't talk about something you don't understand." He brought his voice back down, but his tone remained just as deadly. "My ultimatum still stands. You end things with Titan, or I'll destroy her."

I shook my head. "I'll give you anything else except that. Seize all my businesses. Take my cars. Take my yachts."

"Money means nothing to me," he whispered. "An eye for an eye."

"This isn't an eye for an eye," I snapped. "I didn't take Mom from you."

"No." He slammed his hand on my desk. "But you took *you* away."

I stopped breathing as I stared at the ferocity in his

eyes. His expression slowly softened into a look of abject pain. It was almost difficult to look at.

"You're my oldest son. And you took him away from me."

"I didn't—"

"Choose, Diesel. Break it off with her in the next forty-eight hours, or the world will know about your affair. And if you think you can carry it on without me knowing, think again. I have ten different men tailing you at all times." He turned around and walked to the door, his rage still filling the entire room. It was a different kind of anger, a kind mixed with heavy pain. He stopped at the door and turned around.

It seemed like he might say something, whether it was harsh or soft. But his stare continued with no words. He finally opened the door and walked out, buttoning his suit as he went. He didn't look back.

But I kept watching him anyway.

MY FATHER FORCED MY HAND, AND I HAD NO OTHER choice.

I had to tell Titan everything.

I thought I had more time to figure this out, to convince her to choose me, but now I had to apply the pressure. She needed to make her decision now. She had to end things with Thorn publicly and choose me.

It wasn't ideal.

She wouldn't like it.

But it had to be this way.

When the workday ended, I headed straight to Titan's penthouse. I didn't hit the gym like I usually would, and I didn't change out of my suit. The elevator doors opened, and I stepped inside.

Her shoes were next to the couch, and her satchel was on the table. She must have just walked inside minutes before I did.

"Baby?"

She emerged out of the hallway, in a black dress with three-quarter sleeves. Without her shoes, she was four inches shorter, but it didn't distract from her powerful presence. A gold bracelet was on her wrist along with a matching necklace. Her eyes landed on me, roaming over my expansive shoulders as she crossed the room and headed to me. "This is a nice surprise..."

If only she knew.

I could blurt out everything right then and there, but now that I was looking at her beautiful figure, I decided to be quiet for a few more minutes. My volatile attraction to her always made me lose my train of thought.

She grabbed my shoulders and lifted herself onto her tiptoes to kiss me.

I kissed her back, my hands squeezing her hips. My stubble brushed against her mouth, and I felt her perfume sear my senses. Time seemed to stop anytime I kissed her. I could feel my own pulse in my neck. I could feel my body come alive, burning everywhere as I enjoyed the innate chemistry we shared.

All my anger faded away.

I had nothing to worry about. I believed in what we had. I would tell her my father's ultimatum, and she would choose me.

It would be that simple.

Our kiss lasted a minute, a long greeting between a man and a woman. My fingertips explored her body, feeling her petite waist and the gentle grooves of her ribs. I pulled away slightly and looked into her gaze.

Her lips were slightly parted like she didn't want our embrace to stop.

I never wanted our kiss to stop. "There's something I need to tell you."

Her hands trailed down my arms until they rested on my forearms. "Alright."

"My father stopped by my office."

The desire in her eyes faded away. She instantly shifted, her attitude changing once she realized the severity of the situation. "That doesn't sound good."

"It's not. He gave me an envelope full of pictures of the two of us."

Her face turned stark white, the blood draining from her cheeks. It happened instantly, quicker than the snap of a finger.

"There was a picture of us kissing in the hallway at the gala...among others. He's captured me entering your building late at night...you leaving mine. He'd been tailing us for a while."

"Fucking asshole."

I had worse words to describe him.

"What does he want?" She got right to the point, knowing he wouldn't be tailing us unless there was a reason he wanted dirt on us.

"He's going to show everything to the press unless I stop seeing you." I looked into her fiery green eyes and didn't feel afraid. The conversation would be painful, but we would get through it. She would choose me. I didn't have any doubts anymore.

"What?" she asked incredulously. "What does he get out of that? What's the point?" I shrugged. "He wants me to suffer...and he knows you're the most important thing to me."

She shook her head and crossed her arms over her chest. "I can't believe that."

"He said a few other things to me...that I took myself away from him. That's why he's upset."

Her eyes softened, but only slightly. "I knew it."

"But that doesn't matter. If he really wanted to be on

speaking terms again, he should go about it a better way. He doesn't want to reconcile. He just wants revenge for what I did to him."

"So, you think he's not bluffing?"

I shook my head. "He's definitely not bluffing. He said I have to break things off in forty-eight hours. He'll know if I followed through." There was probably someone watching the building right now. Thankfully, all the windows were tinted, so no one could see us inside.

She stepped back and tucked her hair behind her ear, showing an emotion no one else had ever witnessed from her—fear. She was unnerved by all of this, sick to her stomach. It was my initial reaction too, but I couldn't reveal it to my father. "Fuck."

"I'm sorry he brought you into this."

She paced back and forth, her arms crossed tightly over her chest. "Unbelievable."

"I know."

She paced for another minute before she came back to me. She stopped in front of me, her face tilted to the floor. She breathed shakily, the distress hiding the beautiful features of her face. "I'm not ready for this to end yet…"

Both of my eyebrows rose slowly. "It's not going to end."

"Now right now…but it will tomorrow."

What? Was she serious? "You're kidding me, right?"

She shifted her eyes back to me, her expression full of the torment in her heart. "What other choice do we have?"

The obvious choice. My rage started to simmer under my skin, making me scalding hot everywhere. Like someone dumped boiling water all over me, I burned from the inside out. My hands tightened into fists because I had no other outlet to express my rage. "You choose me, Titan. That's our choice."

The blood drained from her face again. A thin film of moisture covered her eyes. "Hunt, I told you—"

"You told me not to let you go."

"What...?"

"The other night when you were drunk, you told me you didn't want to lose me. You said you didn't want to let me go. You told me you didn't want to marry Thorn so soon because you couldn't walk away from me yet. And now you're ready to walk away from me tomorrow?" Losing my temper wouldn't help the situation, but I couldn't control it. My patience was officially gone. I'd been a dirty secret for too long. I put up with the nightmare only because I loved her so much. I understood her fears, her trust issues. I even understood how guilty I looked. But now I was strung too tight. I couldn't keep doing this anymore.

"I'll never be ready to walk away from you...as long as I live."

"Then. Be. With. Me."

"I told you I was going to marry Thorn. I said that when we agreed to keep seeing each other."

"Then change your mind," I snapped. "You don't have to do anything you don't want to do. If you don't want to marry him, don't."

"You know that's now how it works."

"Yes, it does," I hissed. "End it with Thorn. Step out with me. And that's the end of the story."

"And betray my best friend?" she asked incredulously. "I can't do that."

"Talk to him."

She shook her head. "Hunt, I can't do that. I made my decision, and I have to stick to it. It's a commitment."

I stepped back, my shoulders so tense the muscles started to hurt. "I've done everything for you, Titan. I've sacrificed so much...shit you don't even know. I'm tired of being a lie. I'm tired of being a secret. If you really loved me, really trusted me, you would know I'm innocent. You would choose me, and that would be the end of the story." There was no point in telling her about Megaland because it wouldn't change anything. I'd already given her everything that I had, and it still wasn't enough. Nothing would ever be enough for this woman.

The tears welled and turned into drops.

"I'm sick of this bullshit, Titan." My love for her wasn't enough anymore. I was disappointed in her. I respected her pragmatism. I respected her for being cautious. I even respected her for ending things with me in the first place. But after everything we'd been through, all the long nights of making love, I couldn't believe this was her decision. "I'm not doing it anymore. I've already given you all of myself...and now I don't have anything else to give."

Tears rolled down her face, one of the few times I'd seen her cry. "You know I love you..."

"You don't love me enough."

"Don't say that to me. You were the one with the files in your drawer. You were the one caught kissing some woman. You were the one caught red handed. If that had never happened—"

"I didn't do it, Titan. In a relationship, there is trust. You need to trust me. Would you love me so damn much if I were really a liar?"

No response.

I'd never love another woman as long as I lived. I believed you could fall in love more than once, but if it took me thirty-five years to fall in love for the first time, it was unlikely it would ever happen again. This was it for me. It was either Titan, or it was no one. I didn't want to walk away from this, even now. But I wasn't going to settle for less than what I deserved. My patience had reached a breaking point.

She was still quiet, tears streaming down her face.

"This is it, Titan." I kept several feet in between us, the kind of distance we only showed when we were in public. We were already divided even though I hadn't walked out yet. We were over before the words had officially been said. "We're in this together. Or we're apart. It all depends on you. If you want to marry Thorn, fine. I'm not gonna chase you anymore. I'll move on with my life, go back to a different woman every night as I try to forget about you, and you'll be in a loveless marriage. We'll both be miserable. But if that's what you want, I'm not gonna fight it anymore."

Her eyes shifted back and forth as she looked into mine, the tears pooling at her chin before they fell to the floor.

"Or we could be together. We could tell Thorn what we want. He might be upset, but he'll understand. You guys could announce your split amicably before my father even has a chance to do anything. Then we could be public. People might think we were seeing each other when you were with Thorn, but who gives a fuck? Maybe my father will release those pictures, and the world will see them. So what? We'll be happy, and that's all that matters. I don't give a shit about my reputation, and you shouldn't give a damn about yours—as long as we have each other."

More tears emerged from her eyes, the intensity quickening. She didn't release a sob or change her breathing, but she was still torn into pieces. Her arms tightened over her chest, and she seemed smaller than usual. The powerful woman I knew was fading right before my eyes. She struggled right in front of me.

"Pick me, Titan. We'll figure it out—together."

When she severed our eye contact, I knew her answer. "I can't, Hunt."

I was stupid to think she would give a different answer. The decision filled me with more pain than I anticipated. Tears didn't appear in my eyes, but I felt like I'd just shed a million tears. My chest hurt. All my muscles ached. I felt winded even though she didn't lay a hand on me. I'd been stabbed in the front and the back —at the exact same time.

I was heartbroken.

She quickly wiped the tears off her face and sniffled. "There are so many reasons why I can't..."

"I don't want to hear them again." My body suddenly shut down because that was all I could do to cope. The pain was too much, and I had to protect myself as best I could. I felt betrayed and gutted. There was nothing I could do to prove myself because Titan had her mind made up from the beginning. She was too afraid to trust me—to look past the evidence and have faith in me.

I deserved better than that.

I understood her reasoning, but I didn't agree with it.

There was no going forward.

It was just over.

I didn't kiss her goodbye. I didn't take her bed one last time.

It was the first time I didn't want her.

I gave her one final look in the eye, knowing it was the last time I would ever look at her this way. Until I stepped inside that elevator, she was still mine. She was still Tatum. But tomorrow, she would just be a business partner. She would just be another suit in the board-room. She wouldn't be my friend anymore because I'd never wanted her friendship. I wanted all of her—or nothing. "Goodbye, Tatum."

She took another deep breath, the pain heavy in her eyes. When I disappeared into the elevator, she would sob. I could tell just by looking at her. But despite that pain, she wouldn't ask me to stay.

I held her gaze for another moment before I finally turned my back to her. I hit the button and waited for the elevator to arrive, knowing she was still standing behind me. The minutes seemed to stretch on forever. Finally, the doors opened and I got inside.

I hit the button and stared at the floor.

The doors finally closed.

And the weight of the end hit me. The elevator began its descent to the lobby, and I felt my stomach tighten in misery. Pain bubbled in my throat, and I couldn't swallow the burn. My tongue felt too big for my mouth, and the grief choked me. Every breath I took didn't seem to be enough.

I recognized the sensation because I remembered the last time I felt it.

When my mother died.

But unlike then, I didn't cry.

I did my best not to, refusing to let her break me.

But the burn reached my eyes, the moisture threatening to saturate my face.

I closed my eyes, took a deep breath, and forced the emotions to disappear. I forced myself to straighten, to square my shoulders like a man. I loved Titan with all my heart, really loved her. I wasn't just losing a woman. I was losing the one person who meant the world to me. But I couldn't let that shake me. I had to be strong, to carry on. She wasn't worth my tears, not when she wouldn't choose me.

When the doors opened in the lobby, I'd conquered my emotions.

I was ready to go on.

And hope I would find happiness again...someday.

10

TITAN

MY PENTHOUSE WAS quiet for the next few days.

There was no music. No TV. It was just me, surrounded by four walls of complete silence.

And my painful thoughts.

They never stopped.

They haunted me, like ghosts in an old mansion. They followed me everywhere I went, suffocating me until I couldn't fight them anymore. I cried in the shower a few times. I stuffed his old t-shirt into the back of my closet so I wouldn't have to look at it again. I couldn't sleep because my thoughts wouldn't even stop there. When I drifted off, his face came into my vision, and I was jolted awake again.

I wanted to drink—a lot.

But I promised Hunt I wouldn't. And just because we

weren't together anymore didn't mean I would break that promise.

I could allow myself one drink every few hours, but I knew I wasn't strong enough to pace myself. The second the liquor touched my lips, it'd be all over. I'd drown myself in more alcohol than I did last time.

Hunt wouldn't like that.

I sat on the couch in the dark with my laptop on the coffee table. I should be working, but I couldn't focus. I didn't go into work for the last five days. I had no idea if Hunt came by Stratosphere or not. Maybe he did but knew I needed space. Maybe he didn't and assumed I was working like I usually was.

Letting him go was the hardest thing I'd ever had to do.

Somehow, it worse than losing my father.

I wanted to believe every word Hunt said, and a part of me did. A part of me wanted to forget everything that happened and just start over. But I made a promise to Thorn. If I broke it, it would hurt our relationship. There was no way I could walk away without making him look like a fool to the entire world. I couldn't do that to my best friend, especially when I was leaving him for someone who may have potentially betrayed me.

Thorn never betrayed me.

It would be an insult to a decade of friendship.

So I didn't ask Hunt to stay. I let him walk away, and once the elevator doors were closed, I grieved.

I cried like it was my father's funeral again.

Thorn contacted me a few times, but I always brushed him off and said I was busy. We usually saw each other a few times a week, whether it was just for coffee or dinner. We talked about business most of the time, but lately, we'd been discussing the wedding.

Ugh, I didn't want to talk about the wedding anymore.

His message popped up on my phone. *I just picked up dinner. Can I stop by?*

Thorn was the person I wanted to face the least. If someone else asked how I was doing, it would be easy for me to keep a straight face and pretend everything was fine. But there wasn't a single wall between Thorn and me. When he looked at me, he didn't see my expression —he saw my soul. *Not tonight. I'm wrapped up in a few things.* I tossed my phone aside again, so depressed that I didn't feel the least bit guilty for lying to him.

Thorn's message popped up on the screen. *I'm coming up.*

Fuck, he knew something was wrong.

My hair was pulled into a messy bun because I hadn't showered in a few days. I was in baggy sweatpants and a t-shirt with a chocolate stain on it. I was a complete mess, not prepared for any guest.

The doors opened two minutes later.

I rose to my feet with dread in my chest. I didn't want to do this. I didn't want to face him and say the painful words out loud.

Thorn walked inside without a plastic bag of food. Maybe he'd lied about dinner altogether. Maybe he was just fishing for a reason to see me. He looked me up and down, eyeing my disgusting clothes and greasy hair. He stopped in front of me, and instead of making a smartass comment about the way I looked, he hugged me.

I rested my face against his chest and closed my eyes.

His strong arms wrapped around me, and he squeezed me tightly.

It was nice not to be alone. It was nice to share the air with someone, to feel the pulse of another human being. He shared the pain with me even though he had no idea what crippled me.

His hand moved up and down my back, and he rested his chin on my head. "Tell me what happened. Tell me you're alright." His voice was steady, but there was a hint of genuine terror in his tone. I knew he feared something worse was wrong since I never fell apart like this. The last time I did, I buried my father.

"I'm not sick or anything like that..."

He released a heavy sigh and squeezed me harder. "Oh, thank god. You scared me..."

"I'm sorry."

"Then what is it?" He pulled away so he could look me in the eye.

I didn't want to meet his gaze. I was never afraid to make eye contact with anyone, but now it was too difficult. I focused on his chest, the cotton fabric of his t-shirt. "Hunt and I stopped seeing each other. It's over..." The second the words were out of my mouth, my eyes watered. I took a deep breath and tried to subdue the emotion, but it was too difficult to control. My breath was shaky and the tears bubbled over. Now that I'd said the truth, it was even more painful to swallow.

"Titan..." His hands moved up and down my arms, rubbing me gently. "I'm sorry."

I sniffed before I nodded. "I've been taking it really hard..." I felt pathetic for falling apart so severely. I'd known losing him would shatter me, but I'd never anticipated this kind of destruction. The love I had for him reached far beyond the moon and stars. Even now, I still pictured having his son. A son that looked just like him.

"What happened?"

I had to steady my breathing and my tears before I could speak again. "His father had pictures of us, and he threatened to send them to the papers if Hunt didn't break up with me."

"What?" Thorn's voice immediately rose. "Why?"

"He just wants revenge..."

"Then what happened?"

"Hunt told me...said I should end things with you and be with him. He said we shouldn't care about our reputations and just be together. I couldn't do that so...he walked out. And that was it." I kept my eyes focused on Thorn's chest, knowing I couldn't look at him. I would see his pain reflected back at me, his pity.

"I'm so sorry, Titan."

"I know you are." I knew it killed Thorn anytime I was unhappy. He carried my pain with me, always making sure I never felt alone. He was a hard and cold man to the world, but with me, he was sensitive and compassionate. He was the greatest family I ever could have asked for. I didn't want to live without Hunt, but I couldn't live without Thorn either.

He brought me back into my chest and held me again. "It's gonna be alright. I know that doesn't seem possible right now...but it will. Don't forget who you are. There's nothing you can't overcome, nothing you can't do." His hand moved down my back gently, between my shoulder blades. "And I'm always here."

"I know..."

I DIDN'T GO BACK TO THE OFFICE FOR A WEEK.

I took care of things from home, rescheduled all of my meetings, and sat on the couch a lot. Thorn stayed over almost every night of the week, sleeping in the guest bedroom. We ate a lot of pizza and ice cream.

It wasn't healthy, but it was better than booze.

When I returned to work, I still felt like a mess. But I couldn't miss any more days. I had to run my empire and save the heartache for after work. Once it was past five, I could put on my sweats again and stare at the ceiling.

When I went to Stratosphere later in the day, my heart was in my throat. I was terrified to look at Hunt, not because I thought he would mention our relationship, but because I missed him so much. I might burst into tears at the sight of him.

I stepped onto the floor and walked past our assistants like usual. I didn't even glance in the direction of Hunt's office to see if he was there. Being absent for seven days was a direct confession of my misery, but now I had to be dignified once more.

Jessica followed me into my office. "I've placed all of your messages in this folder along with your schedule." She set the manila folder on the desk.

"Thank you." I set my satchel down and opened it. "Is Mr. Hunt in?"

"No. He hasn't been in all week."

I hid my reaction, like that information meant nothing to me. Maybe he was sitting on his couch all week just the way I was. I couldn't picture Hunt eating ice cream straight out of the carton like I did, but he may have been just as miserable.

"But he left this for you." She placed another folder on the desk. "Let me know if you need anything else." She walked out and closed the door behind her.

I stared at the second folder, almost too scared to open it. My hands were shaky and my pulse immediately quickened. Whatever was inside must pertain to the company, but he also didn't want to have a face-to-face conversation with me about it.

I finally opened it and read the note.

TITAN,

In the pursuit of other interests, I've decided to sell my ownership of Stratosphere back to you. You'll be the sole owner and chief operator of the company, and I'll be reimbursed for my investments as well as the profits for this quarter. My legal team is ready to complete the transaction whenever you are.

SINCERELY,
Diesel Hunt

MY HAND SHOOK AS I HELD THE THICK PIECE OF PAPER.

Our beautiful relationship and unbridled passion had been reduced to professionally written notes with no emotion whatsoever. He was severing ties with me completely—so he'd never have to see me again. Now, this breakup felt even more potent than before.

The tears started back up again.

But I swallowed them, doing my best to keep them buried deep below the skin.

After spending twenty minutes regaining my composure, I picked up the phone and called him. At first, I called his cell phone, but then I realized that was no longer appropriate. I hung up and called his office line instead.

Natalie put me through.

He answered professionally, crisp and cold just like his note. "Hello, Titan. How can I help you?" There wasn't any affection hidden within the words. As if the past six months had never happened, we were wiped clean. All our memories had been scrubbed away.

It took me a moment to process his indifference, to let my heart absorb it without breaking all over again. "I got your memo."

"Name the time and place so we can get it taken care of."

I hated this. I hated his indifference. It hurt more than his disappointment. "I don't think it's fair that you're the one who has to sell. Perhaps I should be the one to relinquish the company to you." We owned it together, fifty-fifty. Just because I was the woman didn't mean I should get the better deal.

"That's nice of you to offer."

His stiff politeness was worse than him being rude. I hated it.

"But I decline. I'll arrange for my team to come by tomorrow afternoon. Would that be alright with you?"

It didn't feel like I was talking to Hunt at all, but a completely different person. "Yeah."

"Then I'll talk to you then. Goodbye, Titan." He hung up without hearing me say anything in return.

That was what our relationship had been reduced to —absolutely nothing.

I WAS IN THE CONFERENCE ROOM WITH MY LAWYERS WHEN Hunt walked inside.

In a black suit and tie, he looked crisp and handsome. His jaw was cleanly shaven, his eyes had a natural light, and his shoulders looked even broader than usual. It didn't seem like he was having sleepless nights. It didn't seem like he was drowning in misery over this breakup. He seemed perfectly fine.

Did he think the same thing of me?

I was dressed in a new outfit, my hair was done, and

my makeup was fresh. But that couldn't disguise my heartache. If he looked me in the eye, he would see my misery. It was there, and it wasn't as if I was trying to hide it.

Hunt walked over to me, his hand extended.

I almost didn't know what to do.

Then I remembered. I shook his hand and cleared my throat, feeling the lack of chemistry between us. Anytime I breathed the same air as him, the attraction sparked like a fire in the hearth. But now there was nothing.

He looked me in the eye, his features guarded by walls and towers. He was hiding everything from me, keeping me locked out of his castle for good.

But if I looked hard enough, I could see it. I could see his pain, his heartbreak.

I knew he could see mine too.

We broke apart and moved to different sides of the table. We went through the new contract page by page, signed where we were supposed to, and came to agreements easily. I doubted that either one of us cared about walking away with more assets. We just wanted to get it over with and make sure it was fair.

Once the final piece was prepared, we signed the last page and the team packed up.

They all filed out, and Hunt came around the table to shake my hand again.

I didn't want him to walk away from Stratosphere, not when he was an amazing partner to have. But just shaking his hand was difficult for me, so I knew this was the best thing for both of us. I couldn't see him every day and pretend everything was alright. I knew he felt the same way.

I shook his hand again. "I really enjoyed working with you."

"Me too," he said quietly. "I know the company is in good hands." He lowered his hand and stepped back.

I should just let him go, but I couldn't. The words rolled off my tongue. "I'm sorry...about all of this."

He steadied himself, his eyes trained on me.

"I didn't want it to end this way. You were such an asset to this company, and it'll be a shame to lose you. I wish you didn't have to give it up..."

He moved his hands into his pockets and stared at me with a cold expression. His look no longer contained the deep intensity he used to give me. Those days were long gone. Now he looked at me with anger and disappointment. "It's the second company I've lost in a month, but I'll manage." He turned to the door, silently dismissing me.

The second company he lost? "Hunt?"

He opened the door but turned back to look at me.

"What other company did you lose?"

He kept one hand on the door as he stared at me. His

jaw clenched then unclenched, and his shoulders straightened as if he was defensive. He turned his eyes away to the window, and after a heartbeat, he looked at me again. As if he had a lengthy explanation, he opened his mouth to talk. But then he abruptly closed it, like he changed his mind. "Nothing...doesn't make a difference anyway."

11

HUNT

I DIDN'T WANT to leave Stratosphere.

But seeing Titan every day was far worse.

Just looking at her made my jaw clench. Just smelling her perfume made my shoulders square in an act of hostility. I was angry with her for the decision she made, but I also resented her.

In addition to that, I was devastated.

I spent the first week in a blur. I stayed in my penthouse and watched a lot of TV. I hit the gym longer and harder than usual. I bought a new plane because I thought that would make me feel better, but the excitement wore off in about five minutes.

Now that my most prized possession had been taken from me, I had nothing to live for.

I didn't care how high I was on the Forbes list

anymore. I didn't care about my expensive cars, my international real estate, or any of my other assets. There was no one to impress anymore. To all the other women in the world, I was still a stacked billionaire. They wanted me as much as they did before.

I was so miserable over Titan that I didn't think about my father once. He did something terrible to me, and I didn't feel an ounce of revenge. The only person I was upset with was Titan. She shouldn't have caved to a madman like him. She should have taken my hand and declared our love for the whole world to see.

But she didn't.

Now I was back to my empty life, back to my superficial and meaningless existence.

But I was also different. My relationship with Titan changed who I was. It made me a better man, but now that she was gone, I was also more bitter. I had unresolved anger that I couldn't defuse.

I blamed all of my unhappiness on her.

She did this to me.

I should give it more time, but I was in a rush to move on. So I went out on the town with Mike and Pine. There was booze, women, and music. I had a woman on my lap in the club and another one tucked into my side with my arm draped over her shoulder. They were there to celebrate a bachelorette party, but they were eager to party with us.

I wanted to be photographed.

I wanted Titan to see it.

I wanted to hurt her for hurting me.

After enough drinks and conversation, Mike and Pine broke off with their dates for the evening.

So I took my girls back to my place. With my arms around their waists, I escorted them outside and into the back of my Mercedes. As I hoped, lots of pictures were taken.

Maybe it was the alcohol or maybe it was the anger, but I turned into a spiteful man. I wanted to hurt the woman I loved because she refused to love me. I wanted to show her I was done being her dirty little secret. Other women would kill to be on my arm in public—but she never wanted me.

We headed back to my place. Their hands gripped my thighs, their mouths were on my neck.

I kissed one. Then I kissed the other.

All I thought about was Titan.

Every time I tried to think about the threesome I was about to have, my sexual thoughts turned back to Titan. I imagined the last time I made love to her, how she told me she loved me while I was buried between her legs.

That was the only thing that got me hard.

My driver pulled up to my place, and we were about to get out. The girls were excited, clawing at me to get my jacket off so they could pop open my buttons and get to my bare skin. They were down for anything, even a tag-team blow job.

But I knew what would happen if I went upstairs with both of them.

Nothing.

I would watch them make out for a little while but then get bored of it.

I knew I was doing this for the wrong reasons.

And that made me an ass. A pathetic one.

Eventually, I would be ready to fuck around again. But right now, I was just as in love with Titan as I ever was. The idea of being with another woman didn't sound appealing. I wasn't even aroused because I was too sad and bitter to feel anything similar to desire.

So I said goodnight to the women and had my driver take them home. Then I went to my penthouse.

Alone.

WHEN I SAW THE PICTURE AND CAPTION AS ONE OF THE top stories on Google, I immediately regretted what I'd done.

My arms were around both of them, and I was grinning like I was having the time of my life. Inside, I was devastated and heartbroken, but to anyone looking at the photograph, that didn't seem to be the case.

I knew this would hurt Titan.

Deeply.

What the fuck was I thinking?

My first instinct was to call her and tell her it was just a mistake. I wanted to tell her I went home alone that night. I didn't even jerk off. But then I realized it didn't matter. Whether I called her or not, it didn't change the situation.

She wasn't mine anymore.

This was what she wanted.

So I never made the call.

Natalie spoke to me through the intercom. "I have Vincent Hunt on line one."

Did this asshole ever quit? "I got it." I picked up the phone and hit the button. "What do you want now? You want my bank account information? Sure, let me get it for you. It's 9-3-4—"

"Looks like you took me seriously. It was a smart move because I wasn't bluffing."

"Of course you weren't," I said coldly. "But you shouldn't be proud of that."

Vincent didn't have a response to that.

I was sick of my father's bullshit. I knew I'd started this feud by giving that interview, but I wanted the war to be over. "Titan is gone, and she's never coming back. I'm miserable, so you can give yourself a pat on the back. There's nothing you have on me anymore. So let's go back to pretending the other doesn't exist. I miss those days." Before he could say anything else, I hung up on him.

I never wanted to hear his voice again. The only time I ever wanted someone to mention him to me was the day he died.

And I certainly wouldn't go to his funeral.

Natalie spoke through the intercom again. "Sir, I have—"

"Never put Vincent Hunt through to me again. Do you understand?" I was being a dick to my assistant when I shouldn't be, but piece by piece, my life was falling apart.

"Yes...sir." Natalie cleared her throat. "But I have Thorn Cutler on the line...can I patch him through?"

Now that was a twist. The two of us had nothing to say to each other now that Titan was gone. What could he possibly have to say to me? "Put him through."

"He's on line two."

I hit the button. "Thorn, how can I help you?" Thorn and I had our ups and downs. We disliked each other, then liked each other, and then disliked each other again. The only thing I did like about him was his loyalty to Titan. She would always have him, and that made it easier to let her go. There was always someone there to protect her.

"What the fuck is your problem?"

Both of my eyebrows rose. "Excuse me?"

"Titan called me in tears after your little stunt. Could you be a little discreet? Do you really need to display your sex life for the whole fucking world to see? She just started going to the office again, and now she's back at home again."

I'd already felt like shit the second I saw the picture. Now I felt like the biggest douchebag in the world. There was no excuse I could give for my stupidity. I was just bitter and pathetic. The idea of her crying just made me want to stab my hand with a pen so I could punish myself.

"Hello?" he snapped. "You there, asshole?"

"She hasn't been working?" I hadn't noticed that detail until I replayed what he said in my head.

"No. She stayed home all week. I was there with her. She couldn't even shower, let alone go to work."

Her misery made me happy, but that was only because I was just as devastated. It made me feel less alone. It made me feel like what we had was real.

"And now you're fucking anything that moves again? Wow, that's classy."

"It's not how it looked..."

"Shut the fuck up. Don't give me that bullshit. I'm glad I talked her out of being with you. So many times, she thought about giving it a real try, but I always talked some sense into her. Looks like I was right for doing so.

You're a lying piece of shit, Hunt. If I ever see you in person, I will punch you in the goddamn face—"

"I didn't sleep with either of them. I kissed them, but that was it. I did it because I wanted to hurt Titan...after the way she hurt me."

"Absolutely pathetic."

"I know I am..." I swallowed the lump in my throat. "I'm just as miserable as she is. I don't know how to cope with it."

"Even if I believed you, which I don't, it still wouldn't make me hate you less."

"I—"

"If you have any respect for Titan, keep it quiet." Click.

The line went dead.

12

TITAN

I CRIED MORE NOW than I did when my father died.

Just when I finally got a grip on reality, I saw that picture that destroyed my already broken heart.

Hunt with a woman on each arm, getting into the back seat of his Mercedes.

I didn't see it coming, so it was so much worse.

He'd told me that's what he would do, but I was naïve enough to assume he would wait a while...at least a month. But he jumped right back into his old ways, picking up beautiful women in short dresses.

And fucking them in the bed I used to sleep in.

I couldn't lie—it really hurt.

The elevator doors opened, and Thorn walked inside with two bags of groceries. "Hey."

"Hey."

He headed into the kitchen and put everything away. He'd been stuck to me like glue since Hunt and I went our separate ways. He had a closet stuffed with clothes, and he'd been sleeping here every night as well as leaving for work with me in the morning. He'd basically turned into a roommate.

When he finished, he walked into the living room and looked into my eyes, checking to see if I'd just been crying.

Thankfully, I stopped a few hours ago. "I appreciate all you're doing for me, Thorn. But you really don't need to stay here. I know you have your own life and need your own privacy."

"You are my life." He took a seat beside and crossed his legs. "Don't worry about it."

I hated the look of pity he gave me. I felt weak and pathetic, not the strong woman I'd spent my whole life building. "You're sweet...but I mean it."

He patted my thigh. "I know you do. And seriously, don't worry about it. There's nowhere else I'd rather be than here with you." He gave me an emotional expression, one full of sincerity and love.

Losing Hunt was agonizing, but I was grateful I still had Thorn. "Thanks."

He pulled his hand away then grabbed the remote. "Want to watch the game?"

"Sure." Sports were safe. Nothing romantic about them.

He turned it on and rested his arm over the back of the couch. "I called Hunt and gave him a piece of my mind." His eyes remained on the TV, speaking casually even though there was nothing casual about what he said.

"What?"

"I told him off and said he was an asshole."

I covered my face in embarrassment even though Hunt couldn't see me. "What were you thinking? Why would you do that?"

"He was a dick, and I had to call him out on it. He's a piece of shit."

I didn't want Hunt to know how much it hurt me, and Thorn obviously told him. "Ugh..."

"He said he did it on purpose to hurt you, but then couldn't go through with it and took them home."

My heart immediately lightened with ease. The last time I saw him, I knew he was angry with me. I could see the rage in his eyes, the frightening aggression. It was difficult for him just to shake my hand. It seemed plausible, and after how close we'd been, I found it hard to believe he would screw someone else so soon.

Thorn turned to me and spotted the relief on my face. "You actually believe him?"

"Yes...is that stupid?"

He shook his head, but he didn't insult me for my words. "It's not stupid. It's just...I don't see why you believe him."

"We really had something. I find it hard to believe he would sleep with someone else that quickly."

"But he went out and picked them up in the first place."

"And he didn't go through with it."

Thorn turned his gaze back to the TV. "I guess it doesn't matter now. I still felt better for telling him off."

"Did he say anything else?" The hardest part about breaking up was moving forward. My heart wanted to stay stationary, to reminisce about our time together. I remembered the heat and passion like it just happened yesterday. A part of me kept hoping for something more, but there was no reason to hope. There was nothing Hunt could do to change our situation. If I wanted something to change, I needed to do it myself. But I couldn't.

"Said he's as miserable as you are."

That shouldn't make me happy, but it did. It made me feel less alone.

Thorn turned back to me, pity in his eyes. "There's no harm in believing him if it makes you feel better. But I hope it doesn't hold you back from moving on."

I couldn't imagine another man in my bed. I couldn't imagine making an arrangement with someone new. I didn't want to kiss anyone, touch anyone, or let anyone touch me. Maybe I would never move on. Maybe I would only have Thorn—and that was it.

I WAS IN MY OFFICE WHEN THORN CALLED ME.

"Did you see the article about Megaland?" There was no introduction at all. He got right to the point.

"No." As I spoke to him, I turned to my computer and typed Megaland into the search engine. "What's going on?"

"Apparently, Vincent Hunt acquired it discreetly a few weeks back."

The page popped up, but I didn't read the story. My mind was too focused on what he said. "What?"

"I couldn't believe it either."

I clicked on the article and started to read while Thorn stayed on the phone.

It's been confirmed that the up-and-coming electronics company Megaland has been quietly acquired by a new owner. Vincent Hunt is now the new CEO of the company, sharing rights with three original creators. Diesel Hunt wasn't available for comment, and it's unclear what sparked this transaction. According to our sources, Vincent and Diesel Hunt despise each other as much as ever. So why would Diesel Hunt sell a company he so recently purchased?

When I finished reading the article, I skimmed through it again. "Hmm..."

"We're missing something here. Why would Hunt sell his company to his father? Even if the company weren't doing well, he still wouldn't do business with him."

"I agree."

"And Hunt believed in that company. He mentioned it to me a few times."

"It was his baby," I said quietly, still thinking quickly.

"Then what's your take?"

I considered the possibilities in my mind while still staring at the screen. "It happened a few weeks before Vincent blackmailed him. Makes me wonder if Vincent blackmailed him again."

"For what?" Thorn asked.

"I have no idea. But whatever it was, it must have been really important to Hunt. He wouldn't have sold that company to his father unless he absolutely had to."

"True. I wonder if it has anything to do with you."

I suspected it did. "I have to go, Thorn."

"Are you going to talk to Hunt about it?"

I remembered the last thing Hunt ever said to me. He mentioned he'd lost another company. When I pressed him on it, he didn't give me an answer. This must have been what he was referring to. "Yes. But a different Hunt."

VINCENT HUNT'S OFFICE WAS SLEEK AND WHITE. EVERY wall was white, and every desk was the same plain color. It was open, airy, and modern. It was rigid and sleek, hinting of the future rather than preserving the perks of the past.

His taste strongly differed from his son's.

I checked in with the assistant and patiently waited for permission to enter his office. Vincent Hunt wouldn't turn me away, not when I was so well connected to his son. Or maybe he assumed I would be pissed about the photographs so he would avoid me. But that was the cowardly thing to do, so I doubted it. I learned that the Hunt men weren't afraid of anything.

Finally, the assistant gave me permission to step inside.

I strutted into that office like a woman on a mission.

It was like the rest of the building, sleek and white. He had a corner office, so half of the room was made of enormous walls of glass. Skyscrapers shone under the light of the sun in the distance. It looked like a throne overlooking the hill.

Vincent Hunt sat behind his desk, atop a gray leather chair. He stared at me with a slightly amused expression, clearly surprised to see me but not put off by it. He held a pen between his fingertips, jet black and shiny. Documents were spread across his desk like he'd just been signing them before I paid him a visit.

He set the pen down and rose to his full height, standing well over six feet like his son. "Tatum Titan. To what do I owe the pleasure?" He didn't walk around his desk but leaned forward to shake my hand.

I disregarded the gesture. "This won't be pleasurable, Mr. Hunt. But I'm sure you already knew that." I straightened the back of my dress before I sat down and crossed my legs. I hadn't been intimidated by this man before, and I wasn't intimidated now. He had pictures of me and his son somewhere in that desk. Kissing, touching, possibly naked. I should be embarrassed, but I wasn't.

A smile stretched his lips, the same handsome one his son possessed. "Even when you intend to be rude, I enjoy your presence. It's refreshing. You're graceful and elegant, but you spit fire at the same time. Doesn't surprise me that my son is in love with you. I'm sure a lot of men are."

I understood people well, but I didn't understand Vincent Hunt. He seemed to respect me, but yet, he wanted to destroy me. All to get vengeance against his son, a man who just wanted his father to be kind to his stepbrother. "I don't enjoy your presence at all. It's difficult for me to be around someone as vile as you." I wasn't afraid of this man, so I wasn't afraid to issue any insult I wanted.

His smile slowly faded away. "I understand you're upset about the photographs. Anyone would be."

"I'm not here to talk about the photographs. Couldn't care less about them."

It was hard to catch Vincent Hunt off guard, but he arched an eyebrow in confusion. He rested his elbows on the arms of his chair and brought his joined hands toward his chest. "Then what's the reason for your visit."

"Your son."

Vincent immediately turned cold, his facial expression callous. "What about him?"

"Your son is a wonderful man. He's kind, compassionate, and I love him with everything that I have. He doesn't deserve to be treated so coldly by his own flesh and blood."

His eyes narrowed, his anger rising a notch. "You shouldn't talk about family affairs that you don't understand."

"But I do understand, Vincent. Diesel can barely speak of you without turning hostile. And it's not because you make him so angry—it's because you hurt him so much."

He stared at me with the same brown eyes.

"And I know you're acting this way because he hurt you. Both of you don't know how to process pain, so you don't know what else to do. He dragged your name through the mud when he did that interview. I can only imagine how much that hurt you."

He didn't react.

"He told me about your last conversation. That you're angry with him because you lost your son. Vincent, you haven't lost him."

When he spoke, he was so quiet I could barely hear him. "I have lost him."

"He's not dead. You always have a chance to make things right as long as you're both alive."

He shook his head slightly. "We can't make it right now. Not now. Not ever."

"Why?"

He massaged his knuckles absentmindedly. "We just can't."

"So your response is to destroy his life?"

"I didn't destroy his life. He shouldn't be sleeping with a woman engaged to another man."

"You don't know anything about my relationship with Diesel or Thorn, so don't pretend that you do." I held my finger. "That's the first lesson I'm going to teach you today. Here's the second. By acting this way, you're only pushing him further away. If you have any hope of reconciling with him, you need to end this war. Call a truce."

His eyes shifted away from me. It was the first time he'd looked away when we'd had a conversation. Most of his power was in his natural style of intimidation. But he dropped those tricks.

"I know you love your son."

After a long pause, he turned his eyes back to me.

"You both need to forgive each other and move past this."

"You really came down here today to talk about this?" he asked incredulously.

"Yes."

"Doesn't add up."

"I love your son. I want the best for him."

"I know you went your separate ways. Or the two of you are the best actors I've ever seen."

"Just because we're no longer together doesn't mean I don't love him. Just like the two of you are no longer speaking, it doesn't change the fact that you love him and miss him."

Vincent held my gaze but stopped massaging his knuckles.

"You need to make the first move."

"Why?"

"Because you started this whole thing by turning your back on Brett."

He released a loud sigh, his eyebrows furrowing. "Now it's your turn to stop pretending to know something you don't understand."

"Okay, maybe I don't understand," I said simply. "But

I know you lost the past ten years with Diesel. Do you need to lose another ten?"

His hard features softened slightly.

"I'd give anything to have another ten years with my father. He left way too soon, and it hurts me to see the two of you alive and well but with no contact. Whatever your problems are, settle them."

"I don't think we can."

"Well, you have to. Because you're his father, and he's your son. Diesel tells me you're a man that can make anything happen. So make this happen."

He shifted his chair slightly as he sat up and rested his hands on the desk. "Not so simple, Titan. But I appreciate your effort."

I felt like I'd made a small dent in his exterior. It was nearly insignificant, but it was something. Perhaps Vincent would take my words to heart and reconsider his approach with Diesel. "Did you blackmail him for Megaland?"

His coldness returned once business was back on the table. "Why don't you ask Diesel?"

"Because I want to hear it from you." I couldn't go to Diesel and ask this question now. When I pressured him about it before, he wouldn't talk about it. Now that we weren't seeing each other anymore, I didn't have the luxury of calling him whenever I felt like it.

Vincent brought his fingertips together and regarded me with that comely but cold expression. Age hadn't affected him the way it did others. His features were still sharp and his complexion was vibrant. He must have committed himself to a healthy lifestyle of diet and exercise. I knew Diesel would look the same in twenty years. "Yes."

I needed more than that. "Why?"

"Megaland should have been mine. It was my find, but he took it before I could even have my meeting with the creators."

"Sounds like he was the better businessman," I said coldly. "Shouldn't take it so personally."

He smiled again. "And where do you think he learned it all?"

"The apprentice always becomes better than the master."

"I wouldn't take it that far..."

"And how did you blackmail him?'

His smile faded away. "The same as last time. I told him I would send all those photos to the newspapers if he didn't cooperate." He opened his drawer and pulled out the folder. He tossed it on his desk, and they slid toward me.

I didn't look at them. All I cared about was what he said. My eyes focused on his face, seeing the coldness

Diesel sometimes wore. Now I knew what Diesel had sacrificed to protect me. He gave away his company, which was worth a fortune, just to protect my reputation. He never told me about it, and that was probably because he knew what my reaction would be.

I would have told him not to do it.

I would have taken the hit rather than let him be manipulated by his father.

I rose to my feet without thinking about it, my feet having a mind of their own. "Thank you for your time, Vincent."

"Anything else you wish to discuss?"

I headed to the door, not bothering to look at him.

"You know, the two of us could do big business together."

I turned around in the entryway. "Vincent, when you die, you can't take that money with you."

His arrogant smile slowly faded away.

"But you can take your son's love."

I walked up to Natalie's desk, feeling weak for the first time in heels. I wanted to kick them off and just be barefoot. My first instinct was to march into Hunt's office, but I realized that would be totally inappropriate. "I need to see him."

"Mr. Hunt is in a meeting right now."

"Oh…" I was so anxious that I couldn't wait. But I was sure he was working on something important, far more important than anything I had to say.

"But you can wait here until he's finished."

"Sure…how long will it be?"

"I'm not sure. Mr. Hunt just made a big acquisition, and he's working with a team right now."

It could be hours, then. But I couldn't go back to work, not when I was this anxious. I'd get nothing done anyway. "I'll wait, then."

"Okay. Take a seat."

I took a seat in one of the armchairs and tried to steady my racing heart. It was beating a million miles a minute. My palms were sweaty and my clothes felt too tight. My heels were killing my feet when they normally felt comfortable.

The large doorway behind his assistants led to the rest of the lobby. There were other offices and departments all over the building. He could be on a completely different floor. I stared at the glass doorway and saw a man in a suit head in this direction. He had the same build, and the suit fit him so perfectly.

He walked up to the doorway while scrolling through his phone. His eyebrows were narrowed like he was deep in thought. The stark lines of his face showed the masculine structure of his jawline.

It was definitely him.

He finally put his phone away and opened the door. "Natalie, I need you to find everything I have on the—" He stopped talking when his eyes settled on me. Dark brown and intense, he immediately stared at me like I was the only person in the room. It was the same way he used to look at me. But then it abruptly changed, like he realized what he was doing and deliberately altered his expression. "Titan." He moved around the desks and walked toward me. "You need something?"

I got to my feet, unable to stand tall and perfect like usual. My heart was still beating out of control. "I need to talk to you...but I can wait until your meeting is over."

He stared at my face, examining me with prying detail. He grazed over my anxious eyes, the tightness of my mouth, and the difference in my posture. "Everything alright?"

"Yeah. It can wait."

Hunt must have known that was a lie because he turned to Natalie. "Tell them I'll be there in fifteen minutes."

"Hunt, it's fine—"

"Come on." He moved his hand to my lower back and escorted me into his office. He shut the door, giving us privacy so we could speak freely. He tossed the folder he'd been holding on his desk and turned his full attention on me. "I know there's something wrong. Talk to me." He didn't put feet between us like he did last time. Now it felt the way it used to, when there was intimacy...and more.

My fingertips almost touched his chest, but I reminded myself he didn't belong to me anymore. "I just saw your father."

His eyes narrowed the way they did when he felt threatened. His dark eyes suddenly seemed sterner.

"I asked him about Megaland. He told me everything."

Hunt didn't change his expression, and he seemed angry by the revelation. "I would have told you, but it wouldn't have made a difference. If I told you as it was happening, you would have told me not to do it."

"You're right. I would have."

He moved his hands into his pockets. "Then why are you upset right now? I've sacrificed a lot for you in the past. This isn't any different. That company meant a lot to me, but you...you've always meant more to me than all the money in the world."

My chest tightened just the way it did right before I cried. I could feel the burn in my throat as well as my heart.

His eyes shifted back and forth as he looked at me, seeing the emotion play out right in front of him. "You always speak your mind. But right now, I can't read you. Tell me what you're thinking."

"What I'm thinking... I'm scared."

"That can't be right," he whispered. "Because you aren't scared of anything."

"Things change."

He stepped closer to me, as if I weren't speaking loud enough for him to hear. He cocked his head slightly, the intensity returning to his gaze.

"I'll probably never truly know what happened months ago. I'll never get a suitable explanation for the papers in your drawer. I'll never really know if you went home with that woman from the club. I'll never know if you were the one who leaked my story to the papers, but..."

Hunt held his breath, his jaw clenching.

"But I don't care anymore. I believe you, Diesel. You may not be able to prove it to me, but I trust you. I'll take a leap of faith for you. If I end up regretting it, so be it. But I'm willing to take that risk to find out."

He obviously hadn't been expecting me to say that, because his eyes softened in a way they never had before. His jaw lost its tightness, and his shoulders relaxed and became straighter. The sigh he released was mingled with a soft moan. He pulled his hands out of his pockets and hung his arms by his sides. Both of his hands tightened into fists, but not out of anger.

"I'm scared that I'm too late. I'm scared that I—"

"Never too late." He closed the gap between us and slid his hands across my cheeks. He cupped my face and pressed his forehead against mine. His chest expanded against mine with the deep breaths he took, and the intensity was evident in the gentle tremor of his hands. "I knew you would believe me if I didn't give up."

"When your father told me you gave up Megaland for me...it didn't surprise me. You've done so much for me, Hunt. That made me realize I couldn't let this slip away. It made me realize I do trust you. I don't know who was really behind those attacks, and I'll probably never find out...but I know it wasn't you."

"Baby...that means the world to me." He leaned into me and kissed me softly, an embrace full of tender love and adoration. "You have no idea."

"I'm sorry that—"

"Don't apologize to me. I understand. I knew this would take time, but I told myself you were worth it. I told myself you would realize the truth on your own. And you have...that's exactly what I wanted."

My arms circled his neck, and I brought him closer to me, feeling my hands and legs shake at the exact same time. "I just had to tell you that. I'm sorry I interrupted your meeting—"

"Nothing is more important than you." He cupped my cheek as he looked into my face. "Nothing."

I kissed the corner of his mouth. "I love you."

"I love you too, baby. So damn much." He rubbed his nose against mine before he pulled away.

"I'll let you get back to your meeting. I just had to tell you that so...you wouldn't make plans with someone else." I didn't want to say those words out loud, but that I needed to get them out. He went out the other night, and I didn't want him to do the same again.

"I kissed them. That was it."

The idea of him kissing another woman made me sick to my stomach, but it wouldn't have happened if I'd believed him sooner. And I knew he wasn't hiding anything from me. If he said that was all he did, that was all he did. He didn't sleep with them. "Okay."

"I'll come over as soon as I'm finished." He kissed my forehead before he stepped away.

"Actually, we can't..."

The love in his eyes died away, immediately replaced by annoyance. "Why?"

"Your father is watching us, remember?"

"You'd better not tell me we're going to be a secret again," he hissed. "Because I'm not putting up with that anymore."

"We do need to be a secret...for a little while."

His arms rested by his sides, thick and tense. He gave me a terrifying expression, his eyes looking like cold dirt. "You'd better have a good reason."

"I have to figure it out with Thorn. I can't throw him under the bus, Hunt."

His anger slowly faded away.

"If your dad releases those pictures, I look bad. But Thorn looks even worse. I can't let that happen."

He finally nodded. "You're right."

"So let me figure that out first."

"Alright," he said with a sigh. "I'll call you when I get home, then."

"Okay."

He gave me a final look before he walked out, and I immediately recognized it.

It was intense, powerful, and full of love.

———

I was lighter than I air, I felt like I could breathe again. The hole that was left inside my chest had finally healed over. My tears were long gone, replaced by my smile. I was taking a major risk by committing to Hunt, especially when there were so many unknowns, but I couldn't keep living apart like this.

I'd rather give it everything and hope for the best.

If he betrayed me again, it would ruin me. I wouldn't be able to get back on my feet after my gut led me in the wrong direction.

But I couldn't stand on my own two feet as it was.

Hopefully, I was right about this.

I sat on my couch in my penthouse and slipped off my heels. There was a kink in the back of my neck, and I absentmindedly rubbed it with my palm. The weight had been lifted off my shoulders, but now I had a new burden to carry.

Thorn.

How would this work?

I'd made a commitment to him, and I didn't see it as anything less than a betrayal for calling it off. He would be upset. I knew he would. I wanted to believe we would still be the close friends we were now, but I really had no idea.

We'd never been in a situation like this before.

My phone rang, and Hunt's name flashed on the screen.

Thorn was immediately forgotten as I took the call. "Hey."

"Hey, baby."

I melted at his endearment. Once upon a time, I told him not to call me that. But now, I loved the affectionate nickname. I loved the way he said it when we were in bed together. It was simple and unoriginal, but it made me feel thoroughly possessed. "I miss hearing you call me that..."

"And I miss calling you that." His masculine voice drifted through the phone and wrapped around me. I could feel his muscular arms securing around my waist even though he wasn't in the same building.

I lay back on the couch and placed my feet on the armrest, feeling my dress slide up as I bent my knees. "I'm sorry, Diesel..." I wished it hadn't taken me so long to come to that realization. Something about Megaland made me understand that I needed to take a chance. Ever since Hunt had been accused of betraying me, he'd been nothing but loyal to me. He'd done things for me, sacrificed so much for me. I couldn't ignore any of that.

"It's okay, baby. Let's forget about it."

"I know I hurt you."

"You have the rest of your life to make it up to me."

I smiled as I stared at the ceiling, imagining the blow jobs in the morning, breakfast in bed, and the other nasty things he'd demand I do for him. "True. Where should I start?"

He answered immediately. "On your back. Legs around my waist. My hand in your hair."

I closed my eyes as I felt the shiver run up my spine. It'd been nearly two weeks since the last time I had him between my legs. It felt like an eternity since the last time I'd had a climax, since the last time I'd had a beautiful man on top of me. "I wish you were here."

"Me too. When this is over, I'm never leaving."

"That sounds nice."

It turned quiet, the two of us silently thinking about

the same thing. My desire for him wasn't just physical, and his need for me was exactly the same. I could sit on the phone with him all night, getting off to the sound of his masculine breathing. I could feel his testosterone through the phone, picturing the way his hands formed fists in irritated restraint.

Time passed, and before I knew it, it'd been ten minutes. I wanted to show up at his penthouse and not care about the pictures his father leaked to the press. I didn't care what anyone thought of me, even if I was a two-timing heartbreaker.

But I could never do that to my best friend.

So I stayed in place.

Hunt spoke after a long, heated silence. "When are you going to tell Thorn?"

Now I was committed to Hunt, but I had to break off my engagement before I could do anything about it. It was a conversation I dreaded, something I wanted to avoid at all costs. The fact that I couldn't have Hunt until it was finished was the only reason I wouldn't procrastinate. "I guess tomorrow..."

Hunt picked up on my sadness. "It'll be alright, Tatum."

It was endearing because no one ever said my first name. Even Thorn never referred to me that way. "I'm not so sure..."

"He loves you. He'll forgive you."

"It's different this time."

"He doesn't like me, but he's not the kind of man to stand in the way. He'll bow out. He's a good guy."

I appreciated the fact that Hunt still respected Thorn despite their differences. "And he would have bowed out. But I made a commitment to him. The entire world thinks this relationship is real. His family adores me. His mother gets tears in her eyes every time we talk about the wedding. It would have been different if I'd called it off sooner, but now it's going to be messy and complicated. Not to mention, I'm going to make Thorn look like a fool."

Hunt didn't brush it off just to get what he wanted. "You're right. It won't be easy."

"It won't be easy at all. I'm so scared I'm going to lose him..."

"It'll definitely be difficult. It'll be painful. But you could never lose him, Titan."

"I'm not so sure. He asked me several times if I was sure I wanted to go through with the engagement..."

"But you didn't know this was going to happen. It wasn't intentional."

"Doesn't matter. He's always been there for me. He's never betrayed me. I don't know how I'm going to hurt someone I love so much..."

Hunt was quiet again, his breathing remaining the same over the phone. "If it were anything else, you would honor that commitment. But since this is the rest of your life, you can't stay just because you promised to. And honestly, you really think Thorn would want that? You think he'd want you to marry him knowing you'd rather be with me?"

The answer was so obvious I didn't need to say it out loud.

"Of course, he wouldn't."

"You're right."

"I'm not going to lie to you and say this is going to be easy. I know it won't be. I can be there with you if it helps."

"No," I said quickly. "It has to be just the two of us. But I'm still scared I'm going to lose him. He truly means the world to me. I wouldn't be who I am without him. He's the one person I can always count on."

"And you can count on him now," he said gently. "And remember, now you have two people you can always count on."

I'D NEVER BEEN SO SCARED TO DO ANYTHING IN MY LIFE.

Even in the face of adversity, I prevailed. When the world was against me, that was the time I really came alive. The more people challenged me, the stronger I became. I prided myself on my fearlessness, on my innate power no one could ever take away from me.

But strength didn't help me now.

This wasn't a business meeting. This wasn't a lawsuit.

This was about one of the two people who meant the most to me.

I couldn't live without him.

He was my family.

I texted him when I got off work, my fingers shaking as I typed my message on the screen. My driver was prepared to take me wherever I wanted to go. All I had to do was give him the order. *Can I come by?*

Sure. Just got out of the shower.

I told my driver where I was headed, and I arrived there ten minutes later. A part of me hoped Thorn would say he was busy, that he had a woman over for the night. But the longer I avoided this conversation, the longer I couldn't be with Hunt. With men trailing us everywhere we went, I couldn't even stop by his office without arousing suspicion. I was stuck communicating with him through a phone when I'd rather be talking through kisses and touches.

I rode the elevator to Thorn's floor and stepped into his living room, feeling weak as if I hadn't eaten all day. Come to think of it, all I had was a piece of toast because I'd been so busy making up for all the time I missed.

Thorn's hair was flat because he hadn't styled it after

he got out of the shower. He was just in his black sweat-pants, and they hung low on his hips. Chiseled as if his body had been carved out of marble, he was in his prime. His fitness was comparable to Hunt's, who was slightly bigger with more veins on his arms.

Thorn was exceptionally handsome, known for his sexy smile as well as his built shoulders. He could have any woman he wanted. We'd been out together, and women didn't seem to care that I was there. They looked at him like they couldn't wait to sink their claws into him.

I seemed to be the only woman on the planet who didn't want him in my bed. The only explanation I could give was the basis of our relationship. He helped me without expecting anything in return, and as a result, he quickly became a brother to me. I'd never shaken off the feeling of family. The idea of being intimate with him didn't bother me because he was a beautiful man. But it would just be physical.

It would never mean anything.

But now, that didn't matter because I wanted to spend my life with Hunt, for better or worse. Thorn wouldn't like the risk I was taking, but he would accept it. But he might never accept this.

"Hey." He approached me at the elevator and gave me a one-armed hug along with a smile. He'd been affec-tionate with me lately since I'd been so miserable over

Hunt. We usually only greeted each other with words and nothing else.

"Hey."

He didn't ask what was wrong because he assumed I was just depressed over Hunt. "Want anything to drink?"

"No, I'm okay." I took off my jacket and hung it up by the door.

"How about some dinner? I can whip up something decent."

"No thanks." I sat on the couch and eyed his cold beer. I'd been doing a tremendous job of steering clear of alcohol. I was proud of myself, honestly.

He sat beside me, facing the TV because the game was on. "How was your day?"

"It was okay. Yours?"

"Same old shit, you know." He rested his arm over the back of the couch and ran his fingers through his hair.

I wanted to sit like this forever, to enjoy the quiet companionship between us. We could say nothing at all, and it wouldn't feel awkward. We could enjoy the silence between us, not unnerved by it like most people were.

Thorn watched the game, having no idea what I'd come there to say.

I felt like shit when I hadn't even said a single word yet.

Fifteen minutes came and went, and then a commercial aired. "It's like they're are throwing the game on purpose..." He shook his head and turned to me, a slight grimace on his face. "I want to buy the team and whip them into shape."

"Sounds like a lot of work."

He shrugged. "It would be a good investment, though. Sports are economy-proof."

"True." Now was my opening to talk to him. The game didn't seem important, and he was making conversation with me just for the hell of it. "Thorn, there's something I want to talk about..." I could barely get the sentence out without my voice shaking.

He focused his eyes on my expression, turning serious the second he picked up on my tone. "What's up?"

It was painful to look into those blue eyes and see only concern for me. I was about to betray him, to give him back the ring I had sitting on my finger. "This isn't easy for me to say. I want you to know that I feel terrible before I even say anything."

He stiffened noticeably then leaned forward to grab the remote. He turned off the TV with a tap of the button then leaned back against the cushions. His muscled torso pivoted toward me, and he gave me that hardened expression he reserved for his enemies. "Give it to me straight, Titan."

My hands came together, and my heart started to

race. "I know I made a commitment to you, but I have to break it. I've decided I want to be with Hunt, that I want to give it a real chance. I know the evidence is still against him, but I choose to believe him. Maybe it'll bite me in the ass later in life...but I'm prepared to take that risk."

Instead of getting angry, he just stared. He didn't blink once, and there was no sign of hostility anywhere else. It didn't even seem like he was breathing. Finally, he looked away and dragged his hand across his chin.

The silence was worse than his screams. "I know you're going to be angry with me, but I want you to know I hate this. I wish I didn't have to do this. I wish there were some other way..."

"You know what we could have done." He stared at the blank TV screen, his jaw rigid. He didn't raise his voice. If anything, it was much quieter. "We could have not gotten engaged in the first place."

He was beyond pissed.

He turned back to me, his eyes burning bright with hostility. "I asked you if you were sure—twice."

"I know—"

"I don't give a damn if you want to be with Hunt, even if I don't trust him. It's your life, Titan. Do whatever the fuck you want. But the fact that you're throwing me under the bus for some guy..." He stood up and shook his head.

"It's not like that." I got to my feet next, feeling my heart race with terror.

"It is like that," he snapped. "Now I'm going to look like a goddamn moron. I lost my woman to Diesel Hunt. That's gonna haunt me for the rest of my life. People are gonna think I'm some kind of dumbass who doesn't know my own girl is sleeping around right under my nose."

"That's not how it's going to look. We'll spin it in a different way."

"In what way?" He crossed his arms over his chest, threatening me with his powerful stance. His arms shook slightly because he couldn't contain all his rage. "There's no possible option that makes me look even remotely good."

"We'll tell the press that we had a mutual split."

"A month after I proposed to you?" he asked incredulously.

"People break up every day. Most marriages end in divorce. It's not that weird."

"No, it is pretty fucking weird." He grabbed a magazine off the coffee table and held it up for me to see. It was a picture of him in a black suit, a close-up of his face. "I just did an interview with one of the biggest fashion magazines in the world. And I went on and on about you and how much I love you..." He ripped the entire magazine in half and threw it on the floor. "This just came out.

Now I'm going to release another statement to the world that we're splitting amicably? Then what happens when Vincent Hunt releases all those photos of you and Diesel? People aren't stupid, Titan. They're going to assume you dumped me because you were sneaking around with Hunt behind my back." He marched off, gripping his skull as he released a quiet scream. He headed to the windows near the dining room, looking across the city so he wouldn't have to look at me.

"Thorn...I'm so sorry." This conversation was going much worse than I had anticipated. It was a nightmare. "I hate this as much as you."

He rested his hands on his hips as he looked outside.

"I understand you're angry and have every right to be...but you have to believe me. I would never hurt you on purpose."

He turned back around, still just as angry as he was a few minutes ago. "I do believe you."

I sighed in relief.

"But that doesn't mean I forgive you."

My heart plummeted into my stomach.

"You forget that I was the one who believed in you first." He slammed his thumb into his chest. "I was the one who helped your first business take off. I've always stood by your side and looked after you. I fucking killed someone for you. You trust me more than anyone else because you know I would never betray you. And now you're destroying everything I worked so hard to build. You're dragging my name through the mud, tarnishing the pristine reputation I've spent my life shaping. Now I'll be seen as a chew toy for Tatum Titan. I'll be seen as a man that some woman didn't want. The world will see that Diesel Hunt is preferable to me. You get to run off and be happy, and I look like the idiot you left behind."

Tears welled in my eyes.

"I would never do that to you." His voice cracked when he spoke, not from tears, but from heartbreak. "Ever."

"I know..."

"You're hurting my parents. You're hurting my family. You're hurting me."

The tears spilled over.

"Be with Hunt. We'll announce our split, and you can have what you want. But you don't get to keep me."

"Thorn—"

"You chose him over me."

"That's not how it is—"

"It is," he hissed. "When you told me you wanted to be with him, I supported you completely. I wanted you to be happy. I wanted Diesel to become part of our weird little family. But now, everything is different. You've been back and forth with him this entire time, and now I'm the one who has to pay for your stupidity."

The sobs started.

As if he couldn't watch me cry, he turned around. "Get out, Titan."

"Thorn..."

He crossed his arms over his chest and stared out the window. His rigid back rose and fell with his deep breaths. He didn't shake, but his aggression filled the air in the room. "I said, get out."

13

HUNT

I HAD JUST finished dinner when Titan called me. I was eager for this news, to know she and Thorn had worked things out. There wasn't a single possibility that Thorn would be able to persuade her to still marry him.

She'd picked me.

But I was worried about their friendship. I wanted Titan to have both of us. He could still be her closest friend and confidant, just the way I had Brett, Pine, and Mike. There was plenty of room for both of us in her life.

Besides, I'd never be able to repay him for what he did for her.

He protected her when I wasn't there for her. I hadn't even met her at the time, but I never would have found her if he hadn't taken care of her. In a way, I owed him everything. I even owed him my life.

They had to make this work.

I answered the phone before the first ring even finished. "Baby."

I was greeted with a quiet sniffle.

And I knew. "Baby..."

She did her best to control her voice, to make sure she wouldn't break down in tears again. But her resistance wasn't enough. Her sorrow broke through. "He won't forgive me..."

"He's just upset right now." If she couldn't make it work with him, then I'd have to take care of it. No way in hell would I let Titan lose the best man in her life—besides myself. She needed him just as much as she needed me. "Give him time."

"It's different this time, Hunt..."

"He loves you. You love him. It'll be alright."

"No..."

"What did he say?"

"He said...it doesn't matter." A quiet cry made its way through the phone. "I'm not a loyal friend to him. I've chosen to humiliate him in front of the whole world when all he's ever done is protect me. I know he's right... I understand how he feels."

"It's more complicated than that."

"He doesn't care that I want to be with you. But he does care that I'm backing out of my commitment to him. He said he would be fine if we just hadn't gotten engaged in the first place, but I'd told him I was sure..."

"And that's how you felt at the time."

"It doesn't matter to him." She started to cry harder. "I don't know what I'll do without him... I don't need him because of the things he does for me. I need him because I love him."

This was killing me. I had to listen to the love of my life cry her eyes out. She wanted to be with me, and as a result, lost her closest friend. My first impulse was to hang up and run to her penthouse as fast as could. I could circle my powerful arms around her and protect her from everything.

But I couldn't do that.

Not without making my father unleash his threat.

Staying still was the hardest thing I'd ever had to do. "I wish I could be there with you."

"I know..."

"I promise it's going to be okay, baby. I'll make it okay."

"I wish I could believe you...but I don't think there's anything either one of us can do. Honestly, I don't blame Thorn for feeling this way. This is entirely my fault. I shouldn't have told him to propose unless I was absolutely sure. If I had just asked for more time, things would be different."

"Don't act like he didn't pressure you, Titan."

"He nudged me...but he never pressured me."

"You're being too hard on yourself."

"I never make excuses for my failures. I take responsibility for my actions. This is my fault, and we both know it is. My love for you clouded my judgment, and I wasn't thinking clearly. I just wish I didn't have to lose my best friend over it..."

"You won't." I didn't know what I could do to fix the situation, but I was definitely going to do something.

For her.

———

THE SECOND I STEPPED INSIDE THE LOBBY, THORN'S assistant stiffed. Her eyes widened, and she watched me like an intruder that didn't belong in the building. "Mr. Cutler told me to dismiss you if you ever stepped inside this office..." Her execution was weak because her eyes trailed down my chest toward the rest of my torso.

I walked past her desk and headed to the double doors that led to his space. "I'll tell him you did your best." I helped myself into his office and found him sitting behind his large desk. In a navy blue suit with a serious expression, he looked anything but pleased to see me. A mug sat next to his computer, but I suspected it was coffee mixed with a little booze. His stern look was enough to chase away anyone else.

Not me.

"I will call security," he said. "I'm not bluffing."

I spotted the cord that connected to the back of his phone, so I yanked it out with one swift motion. "Good luck."

His eyes followed my movements as I lowered myself into his guest chair. His look of displeasure intensified.

Pissing him off wouldn't get me far, but he needed to know he couldn't chase me away. "You know why I'm here."

"I have a pretty good idea." His legs were crossed, and he swiveled his chair slightly back and forth with the foot that was planted against the ground. "But don't expect me to care. I don't know what you said to her to make her flip on me, but you should have been a lawyer. You're a master manipulator."

"I didn't say anything to her. And I'm certainly not manipulating her."

He said nothing, casting his doubt in silence.

"My father blackmailed me into giving him Mega-land. If I didn't hand it over, he was going to sell Titan out to the media. I didn't have any other choice, so I caved. When my father told her that, it finally made her realize that I would do anything for her."

Thorn didn't seem impressed by this news at all.

I was hoping to get some sort of reaction out of him.

"I know you're upset right now, but cutting Titan out isn't the solution."

"I'm not cutting her out," he said coldly. "She's cutting me out. She's willing to ruin my reputation just to be with a man she can't completely trust. She even said to me that she's willing to risk being wrong just to be with you." He tilted his head slightly, his eyes narrowing. "That hurts most of all. She's ruining me just for the possibility to be with you... Shows where her priorities are."

"You're taking it the wrong way."

"I'm not." He rested two fingers against his temple. "I've always had her back, and she's supposed to have mine. Only she doesn't. I'm not going to invest my time and loyalty in someone who won't do the same for me. I'm done."

"You would really rather her honor her commitment to you than be with the love of her life?" I asked incredulously, knowing there was no possibility that was the case.

"I never said she couldn't be with the love of her life. She could fuck you every night, and I wouldn't give a damn. She's had all the freedom she's ever wanted. I've never tried to take that away from her."

"You know she can't be married to you and sleep with me."

"Then that's her problem, not mine."

I knew that was just his anger talking. "Thorn, come on."

"Come on, what?" he asked. "This situation would be completely different if I didn't get down on one knee on live television and ask her to marry me. This conversation would be completely different if I didn't just do an interview with the biggest fashion magazine in the country and profess my undying love for her. The most important thing in the world to Titan is her empire, which includes her reputation. But she's willing to destroy mine because of her own mistake. If it were me, I would honor my commitment in a heartbeat."

"I don't believe that." If Thorn met the love of his life, he would do anything to be with her. "When you meet the right woman, you'll know I'm correct."

He rolled his eyes. "Not every man is a one-woman kind of guy. I'm one of them."

"I thought I wasn't either. Things change."

"And some things don't," he said coolly. "I've already been patient enough with your bullshit relationship. We lost a great deal with your father because she wanted to be loyal to you. I accepted that and moved on. I accepted a lot of things from her. In fact, I would accept anything she threw at me. But this..." He lowered his hand and rested it on the desk. "This is a whole new ball game. Her decision affects my entire life. And she's still willing to do it. She's willing to screw me over to get what she wants."

"She's not doing it to get something," I corrected. "She's doing it because she's in love with me. She wants to marry me, have kids with me."

"And where does that leave me?" he snapped. "I'll always be known as Tatum Titan's pathetic leftovers. I'll always be known as the guy Titan dumped. I told the world I loved her, and then she left me. Then when the world finds out about the two of you, they'll know she was cheating on me. It makes me look like I can't keep a woman satisfied. It makes me look like an idiot."

There was no denying any of that. It would truly affect the media's perception of his character.

"Right now, the world thinks I'm the luckiest bachelor in the world. Not only am I marrying the most beautiful woman in the public eye, but the most successful woman on the planet. That makes me look like a goddamn king. You know how many times my mother has cried over this wedding?"

I held his gaze.

"Now I have to tell her that Titan left me? You have any idea how much this is going to hurt her? Titan's decision isn't just affecting my life. It's affecting the lives of those I love. So how can you expect me to be okay with this?"

"I never said you should be okay with it. But I think you should forgive her."

He clenched his jaw as he stared at me. "Forgive her?

I murdered someone for her. Asshole, I've been the most committed friend on the planet. When the banks didn't give her a loan because of her father's debts, who did? There wouldn't be a Tatum Titan if it weren't for me. I've done everything for that woman, and this is what I get in return?" He slammed his hand down on the desk. "It's cold betrayal—that's what it is."

"I get where you're coming from, Thorn. And no matter what you say to me, I'll always respect you. I'll be in your debt for as long as I live. You protected my woman when I wasn't there for her."

His angry expression refused to soften.

"But she's only doing this because she's just as in love with me as I am with her. If it were anything else, she would be there for you. If you asked her for any favor, no questions asked, she would deliver. But she needs me."

That didn't mean anything to him.

"I'll make this right, Thorn."

"There's nothing you can do," he said coldly. "This isn't about you, Hunt. It's about Titan and me."

"I'll take the bullet for this one."

His eyebrow rose.

"Tell the media you dumped her. Be photographed out with some other woman so the world thinks you've already moved on. Then I'll come into the picture, and I'll tell everyone I'm just her rebound. Titan will go along with it and say she misses you. And she'll say she's just using me. You come out looking good while the two of us look stupid. I fixed your problem."

"Fixed my problem?" he asked incredulously. "I just told the world I'm madly in love with her. Why would I dump her a week later?"

"Say you found someone else."

"So I look like an ass?" he snapped.

"When my father releases those photos, the world will think you did the right thing because she was a cheater anyway. Titan and I will sabotage our own credibility, and you'll walk away with the best reputation."

He shook his head slightly. "That's a terrible plan."

"Wouldn't you prefer to look like an ass rather than an idiot?"

He held my gaze as he considered it. His blue eyes shifted back and forth slightly, his mind working furiously. "I suppose, but it's still a terrible idea."

"It's the best we can do."

"And you're willing to look desperate to be with her?"

I didn't have a single doubt. "In a heartbeat." I didn't care what the world thought of me. I only cared about Titan's opinion. The two of us could avoid the public eye hidden away in our homes. We would be naked and happy. We could work from home until the world forgot about us once more. "Now I need you to forgive her, Thorn. You mean the world to her."

"No, I don't. If I meant the world to her, we wouldn't be having this conversation."

"Thorn, she needs both of us."

"No, she only needs you. She's made that pretty clear."

I'd thought my plan would make everything better, but it didn't seem to make a difference. "Take some time to cool off. I'll stop by again in a week or so." I rose out of the chair.

"Don't bother," he said. "I don't want her in my life anymore. She's not my friend."

I couldn't tell Titan that. "I'm not gonna let this go until I get you two back together."

"Then you're wasting your time."

"Thorn—"

"The fact that I have to lie to my parents and pretend to be an asshole to Titan is the worst part. I'll never forgive her for that."

"Then why don't you tell them the truth?" I demanded. "Tell them it was just an arrangement."

"That the entire relationship was a fabricated lie?" he asked incredulously. "What could my family possibly say to that? Then I would have to give an explanation of why I don't want a real marriage, and that's another can of worms. That alternative is even worse. They'll never trust anything I say after that. I'd much rather let them think I was an asshole than that…"

I couldn't find any common ground with him, and unfortunately, I understood his point of view. Titan had put him in a very difficult situation. I wouldn't pretend otherwise. "I know it's shitty. I know you feel betrayed. But remember the last ten years of you and Titan. You're never going to find another friend like her, and she's never going to find another friend like you. Don't lose each other, not when you need each other the most."

Thorn turned away, severing his contact with me. "I wish the two of you a lifetime of happiness. And I really mean that." He turned his eyes back to me. "I won't be there to protect her anymore, so I hope she's right about you."

I loved that woman with all my heart. If I didn't, I wouldn't be here fighting for her friendship. I wouldn't be willing to sacrifice everything to make this work. "She is."

I waited until I was home before I called her. I could have made the call from my office, but I didn't want to upset her while she was at work. She probably had a few meetings that day, and I didn't want her eyes to be puffy and red.

So I waited until I was home to tell her the dreaded news.

I wanted to sprinkle the conversation with sugar and make it seem better than it really was. I wanted to lie and say everything with Thorn would blow over soon.

After talking with him, I didn't think it would ever blow over.

Could this really be the end for both of them?

I sincerely hoped not.

When I was in the shower, I was tempted to beat off to a fantasy about Titan. I hadn't gotten any action in weeks, and I hadn't given myself a treat either because I was too miserable. But now that Titan had chosen me, my body hummed with life. I wanted to plow into her all night long and all through the day.

But I didn't.

I'd rather wait for the real thing.

I dried my hair with a towel and pulled on a pair of clean sweatpants. Then I called her.

She answered right away. "Hey."

"Hey, baby." I walked into the kitchen and found the meal that my maid had prepared for me. I tossed it in the microwave to heat it up again.

"How was your day?"

She didn't know I went to Thorn's office. I hadn't told her my plans beforehand. "It was alright. Yours?"

"It was...alright." A hint of sadness escaped her voice.

I leaned against the counter and dreaded the conversation we were about to have. Losing Thorn was one of the worst things that could happen to her. All I wanted to do was make her problems go away, but I didn't how I could make that occur this time. "I stopped by Thorn's office today."

She sighed loudly into the phone. "I told you he wouldn't forgive me." She already knew the outcome to the conversation before I even told her about it.

"I'll wear him down, Titan."

Her voice escaped as a whisper. "He's not going to change his mind this time, Hunt. But I appreciate that you tried."

"He's angry right now, but once the dust settles, he'll come around. I know he will."

"What did he say?"

"A lot of things. He basically said he couldn't forgive you for feeding him to the wolves. I tried to tell him that you didn't want to do this, that if it were anything else, you'd keep your promise to him. He didn't see it that way."

She was quiet.

"I came up with a different plan in the hopes of enticing him."

"What plan is that?"

"I told him to publicly dump you and immediately be seen with someone else. As a result, you run off with me as a rebound. I'll even make some kind of statement to corroborate the story. It makes us both look bad."

"And it makes him look like a jerk," she said. "How is that any better?"

"It's better to look like the heartbreaker asshole who left than the idiot who got left. Neither one of them is great, but that's the better option of the two. He agrees."

"And you're willing to look like second best?" she asked incredulously.

I gave her the same answer I gave Thorn. "In a heartbeat."

"What happens when your dad leaks those photos? The world will think I was cheating on him."

"They'll think he did the right thing by dumping you. His reputation will look better, yours will look worse."

"I guess..."

"That was the best I could come up with."

She sighed into the phone again. "I'm going to be America's most-hated woman..."

"You will be." I didn't sugarcoat it. "But people will forget about it once the next big story hits."

"But my image will still be tarnished. It'll be even more difficult to get anything done because people won't take me seriously. I'll have to work three times as hard to be respected. Connor will drop my endorsement, and all the women who looked up to me will no longer see me as a role model..."

"I can promise you no one will give you a hard time once you're publicly dating me. Even if I act like I'm some kind of rebound, people won't cross me. So they won't cross you, Titan."

"I don't need to rely on a man to protect me. Never have and never will. That's not the point, Hunt."

"I know it's not. But it'll still make things easier. As for the shattered image...there's not much we can do that about. But we can certainly rebuild it. If we do enough, we can make the public see you in a different way."

Judging by her silence, she wasn't thrilled by that idea.

"I'll be there with you the whole time. We'll be together, and that's all that matters." I could declare my love to the world, have my arm around her waist anytime I was at a business conference. We'd spent romantic nights together in the bed we shared. We would have exactly what we wanted, a family shortly afterward. I didn't give a damn what people thought of me. I'd gladly trade in my image to be with Tatum Titan.

"I know," she whispered. "It's just...it's a lot harder for me."

She would always be held to a double standard. Men in suits never had to smile during a business meeting, but she had to dress like a supermodel anytime she went anywhere. Otherwise, people would question her skills. I could show up to a meeting in jeans and a t-shirt, and no one would care. Her castle would crumble overnight, all because of me and my father.

I wished I could fix everything. "It'll be hard in the beginning, but it'll get better. I promise."

"You're making a promise you can't keep."

I wouldn't give up until she had everything she wanted. "I can keep this one."

I met Titan at Thorn's office. She was sitting in the waiting room when I got there, her cheeks noticeably pale. Her makeup was pristine as usual, but she didn't display her usual beauty.

She looked devastated.

Her legs were crossed, and her hands rested together on her knee. She didn't hold herself with the same grace she usually possessed. Heartbreak had defeated her, and her eyes were sunken with the weight of her grief.

She didn't even look at me when I walked inside.

I sat in the chair beside her, and that's when she noticed my presence. My hand ached to reach for hers, to grip her with my strength. I wanted to give her all of my power, to make her feel invincible. But all I could do was sit beside her, keeping my hands to myself.

She didn't say anything to me.

I'd never been so happy but so miserable at the same time.

Titan was my finally mine, officially and eternally.

She'd ignored her doubts and committed to me because her heart couldn't let me go. She was risking everything to spend her life with me.

I was the luckiest man in the world.

But watching her misery broke my heart. I wanted her to be happy, to see her eyes light up when I entered the room. I wanted her to love me every single night, but I also wanted her to have the man who meant so much to her. I wanted it to be the three of us—not just the two of us.

Any other man would be jealous and possessive. Any other man would despise Thorn for ever placing a ring on her finger. He'd want to keep her away from him. But that wasn't how I felt at all.

I wanted her to always have him.

His assistant finally ushered us inside, and we entered his office. Thorn sat behind the desk, looking as callous as he was yesterday. He was in a different suit, but he wore it the same way—full of silent hostility. He hardly glanced at Titan before he looked away. "I've thought about what Hunt said yesterday." He didn't even give Titan a chance to speak, like her voice would only irritate him. "I think we should do it. It's the best option."

Titan stopped in front of his desk, looking at him with the kind of love she never showed me. It wasn't full of romantic affection or lustful commitment. It was the same way I looked at Brett. She looked at him like family, like a brother or a father. "Thorn—"

"I don't want to listen to you repeat yourself." He rose from his chair and slid his hands into his pockets. His eyes returned to her face, full of cold venom. "And I don't want to listen to Hunt try to convince me I should forgive you. I don't forgive you, Titan. Nor will I ever."

Fuck, that was harsh.

Titan did her best not to cry, but her eyes noticeably tightened in pain.

"I have to embarrass my parents by acting like an asshole. I have to throw away the powerful and professional image I've built for myself since day one. I have to completely start over and pretend to be something that I'm not—because of you."

Watching this almost made me want to bow out altogether.

"I want nothing to do with you, Titan. When we're finished, I never want to see you again. If we're at the same event, you pretend I don't exist. And I pretend you don't exist."

I understood Thorn felt betrayed, but this was cold. "Thorn, come on. What do you expect her to do?" I walked up to his desk and stood beside her, knowing she was exercising all her restraint to keep a straight face.

"I understand her decision," Thorn said, his eyes on me. "Just as she should understand mine."

My hands formed fists because I couldn't process my frustration. I really thought Thorn would let this go once he voiced all his anger. But he was moving forward without any indication of doubt. "If the situation were reversed, you know Titan would forgive you."

"I'm sure she would. But she doesn't have the best judgment. And that's exactly why this is over."

Titan released the breath she was holding, her pain obvious.

"Thorn, I'll give you anything you want to make this work." I had more money than I knew what to do with and connections that could push his career further. I would drop all of that just to make Titan happy.

His eyes narrowed on my face. "You can't put a price on friendship, Hunt. That's why it's so valuable." His eyes shifted back to her, full of disappointment. "You aren't a friend to me, Titan. A friend wouldn't destroy me like this."

Her voice remained steady, despite the emotion that was choking her. "I'm not doing this on purpose, Thorn. I don't have any other choice. I have to be with Hunt. I can't live without him..."

"And I understand that. It's always been different with him than all the others." He continued to keep his hands in his pockets, acting as if this conversation were far calmer than it really was. "I respect your decision, and I don't see any other option for you. But I'm not going to forget that I'm the victim of your choices. You expect me to sweep that under the rug?"

"No, but I—"

"Ever since Hunt came into the picture, our friendship has never been the same. It's been shaky and unpredictable. I never know where I stand. One moment, you're standing with me. And then the next, you're standing with him. If you hadn't told me to propose, everything would be different—but you did. We can't change that. We can't change what's about to happen."

Titan was finally silent, empty of words, empty of hope.

I didn't see a future for the two of them. I saw the chaotic destruction of a friendship. I saw the deterioration of a family. It was painful to watch, but I couldn't stop staring.

"My team will make the statement this afternoon. I suggest you don't comment until they catch me with some other woman. And even then, I still wouldn't make a statement. Vincent will release the photos, and the fire will just keep burning." He rubbed his jaw as he stared at Titan, looking at her like someone he hardly knew.

All Titan did was give a nod.

"I think that's it," Thorn said dismissively. "Take care." He lowered himself back into the chair and rolled it up to his desk. His hand moved to the mouse, and he immediately gave all his attention to the screen.

Titan didn't move. So I didn't either.

She moved to the edge of his desk and pulled the diamond ring off her finger. With careful fingers, she set it on the surface. A gentle tap filled the large room, the echo of their ending friendship. "If you ever need anything, you can always come to me. I'll always be there for you, no matter what, even if you don't see me as a friend anymore."

Thorn's body stiffened slightly, but his eyes stayed on the computer. The movement was so subtle I wasn't sure it had happened at all.

"I understand your decision, as much as it pains me. But I want you to know that I love you...that I'll always love you. If you ever change your mind, you know where to find me. And I certainly hope you do." She made a bold gesture by placing her hand on his. Both of them rested on the mouse, and Thorn stopped clicking the buttons. He still didn't look at her, but he didn't push her hand away either.

She waited another thirty seconds, hoping he would say something in return. But when it was clear he would keep his silence, she finally let him go. She pulled away and straightened her shoulders before she turned around. Tears swam deep inside her eyes, but she didn't let them emerge. She remained tall and strong, walking out of there with her head held high even though it was the most painful thing she'd ever had to do.

I refused to believe that this wasn't killing Thorn. He was still absorbed in his anger, so he was numb to the pain. He loved Titan, and since I loved her too, I knew watching her suffer was agonizing.

It nearly killed me.

14

TITAN

I DIDN'T CRY ANYMORE because there were no tears left to shed.

It was done.

I lost my friend.

The TV was on in the living room, and the news story played over and over. Reporters dissected Thorn's announcement until there was nothing left to discuss. *"Thorn Cutler made a surprising announcement today when his team stated he and Titan had ended their years-long relationship overnight. Just a few weeks prior, he proposed to Tatum Titan with a gorgeous ring. With tears in her eyes, she said yes. This comes as a surprise to all of us, and it's left more questions than answers. What exactly happened?"*

I grabbed the remote and changed the channel. There was a game on, and I'd much rather stare at that than listen to the world discuss my fake relationship. Thorn's mother called me once, but I didn't answer. She left a message, but I was too much of a coward to listen to it. I had no idea how Thorn wanted to handle the news with his parents, and since we weren't on speaking terms, I couldn't ask.

My phone rang, and Hunt's name popped up on the screen.

I should be happy right now. I should feel my heart sprout wings the second I saw his name on the screen. My guard was down, and my heart was open to him—so were my legs. But it difficult to feel something other than sorrow. Thorn meant just as much to me—in a very different way.

I answered. "Hey."

Hunt's masculine voice sounded even deeper on the phone. I couldn't see his handsome face, so my listening senses were heightened. "Hey, baby."

Baby. I loved hearing that name. It was soothing all the way down my spine. I never wanted him to call me Titan again, not when I meant something more to him than I did to everyone else. "Hey..." Now I was repeating myself like an idiot, but I didn't have the grace to correct myself.

"I want to see you."

Now that the news was out, there was nothing holding us back. Even if Vincent wanted to unleash those pictures, the story wouldn't break until the morning. What we did tonight wouldn't change the outcome of our future. "I want to see you too. But honestly...I'm pretty down. I'm not pleasant company."

"You were never pleasant company," he teased.

A pained smile formed on my lips. "I don't want to start our relationship this way. I want you to know that I'm happy...I am happy. But I'm also absolutely miserable right now."

"I know, baby. So let me be miserable with you."

He always knew the right thing to say.

"I'm in the lobby, standing in front of your elevator. I'm coming up whether I'm invited or not."

"Then why did you call?"

His smile was obvious through the phone. "Wanted to be a gentleman." He hung up.

I was still in my clothes from earlier that afternoon. My heels were abandoned in the middle of the floor, standing upright with utter beauty. I loved shoes as much as clothes, but after wearing them all day, I couldn't handle them anymore. An Old Fashioned was on the table in front of me, but I wasn't ashamed to drink it. I still drank. I just hadn't lost my control over it.

The doors opened and he stepped inside. He wore a thick black jacket to fight the winter cold. He peeled it off and hung it by the door, in dark jeans and a long-sleeved V-neck underneath. It looked wonderful against his fit body, hugging his ripped muscles in all the right places. His jaw was cleanly shaven, which was a slight disappointment. Beard or no beard, he was utterly sexy. But I liked the way his stubble rubbed against my soft skin when he kissed me.

He joined me on the couch, his eyes invading my appearance. They looked over my body, spending the most time on the hollow of my throat. Without placing a single hand on me, he could devour me like a wild animal. After months of screwing him, I thought I would get used to this behavior. But I never did.

His hand moved to my neck, and he leaned in and kissed me softly on the mouth. It was a gentle touch, full of love and affection. While the sexual intensity was there, he didn't push it on me. He restrained himself instead, knowing I wasn't myself tonight. He moved his lips to my forehead next and placed a kiss there.

He could make me feel so loved with an action that was so simple.

I looked into his mocha-colored eyes and suddenly felt warm in spite of the raging winter right outside my window. For just an instant, I felt safe despite my shattered heart. It gave me a brief moment of hope, that I would get through this somehow.

His fingers trailed behind my ear where he tucked in my hair. Then they slid down my arm slowly until they settled on my thigh.

"I'm happy that you're here." I knew he was staring at the sadness in my eyes and seeing a woman who had fallen apart. I wasn't jumping into his arms and letting him carry me to the bedroom. "I'm sorry that I'm not showing it better."

"It's okay," he said quietly. "When you're sad, I'm sad. That's how this is going to go for the rest of our lives."

My eyes softened, and I rested my hand on top of his.

"But I'm sleeping here tonight. And tomorrow night. And the night after that..."

A smile tugged at my lips. "I assumed."

"But I won't make a move on you tonight. I can tell your mind is somewhere else."

"I'm sorry..." I broke eye contact and looked at the ground. "I wish it didn't have to be this way. I wonder if it would have been better if I'd just stayed engaged to Thorn. But I know that would have made me more miserable in the end. When I go over my choices, I wonder if there's something better I could have done. But I don't see another alternative."

"Because there is none." He squeezed my hand.

"That makes me feel better, but only slightly. I'll never get over losing Thorn. I know it's hard to understand. He's been a crucial part of my life for so long. He knows me better than anyone else. It's like...losing a piece of myself."

His hand moved underneath my chin, and he directed my gaze to him once more. "He'll come back."

"You heard him, Hunt."

"Diesel."

My eyebrows rose.

"Don't call me Hunt ever again."

My hand slid up his muscled thigh, feeling his strength through the thick jeans. "Okay."

"I know he'll come back. It might take a few months, but he will."

I didn't want to latch on to hope when it might just slip away. "Why do you say that?"

"Love like that doesn't just die. He's angry right now, but once that pain settles, he'll miss you. The guy killed someone for you...let's not forget that."

"Like I ever could..."

"He'll come back, baby. I know he will."

I was grateful Diesel was so supportive of me. Other men wouldn't be so understanding. "I'm sorry if it seems like I talk about Thorn a lot. I know it must get old. I know it must bother you..."

"It's never bothered me. I have nothing to be threatened by." His hand slid over my neck as he looked at me. "You love me—and only me."

WE LAY IN MY BED TOGETHER, ALL THE LIGHTS OFF AND surrounded by darkness. The lights from the skyscrapers filtered through my tinted windows. At the touch of a button, the shades could come down and seal us in darkness. But I liked the way the lights trickled through the windows sometimes.

Hunt lay beside me, all muscles and all warmth. He was on his side, his head sharing a pillow with me. He hiked my leg around his waist and pressed our chests together. I was in one of his old t-shirts, treasuring it as a relic from our past.

His face was just inches from mine, and he kept looking right at me. As if he could see something more than just my gaze, he stared at me like the universe sat in the center of my eyes. His look was piercing and invading, but I liked being conquered by this man every way possible.

His veined forearm hooked around my waist, his fingers gently rubbing against the bare skin of my back underneath my shirt. Without sharing a single kiss, we exchanged so much passion. I could feel it in the limited space between us. I could feel it in his pulse. I could feel it in the way he looked at me.

We weren't making love, but we almost seemed to be. His gaze washed over me like waves from the ocean tide. It reached every inch of my skin, even the nape of my neck. I felt overwhelmed by his presence, drowned in his possessiveness.

His masculine voice shattered the silence around us. "This is nice."

"It is…"

"I want to do this every night for the rest of our lives."

It was the most romantic confession I'd ever heard him make. "Me too."

"Then we will."

———

Diesel left when my alarm went off. He showered at my place then went back to his penthouse to change.

I walked him to the door and gave him a kiss good-bye. "Bring a bag next time."

He smiled against my mouth. "I'll bring more than that. I'll need a dresser and half of your closet space."

"Uh, I don't know about that. I have a lot of shoes…"

He squeezed my ass with his big hand. "Then get rid of them." He kissed me on the forehead before he stepped inside the elevator. "Love you." He said it casually, just like every husband said to his wife before he went off to work.

It was nice. "Love you too."

He watched me until the doors were closed and he was gone.

I went back into my room and got ready for the day. I didn't dare turn on the news to see what happened next with Thorn. Maybe he'd been photographed with another woman already. Maybe the media had twisted the story in some other ridiculous way.

After I finished getting ready, I turned on the TV.

They were all covering the same story as last night, except Thorn had already been photographed with some woman in a club. He was grinning like an idiot with his arm around her shoulders.

There was no sign of Vincent Hunt's pictures.

I turned off the TV, walked to the elevator, and then stopped in my tracks.

Vincent hadn't leaked those photos yet, but I was certain it was only a matter of time. He was probably getting ready to do that right this minute. Once he arrived at the office, he'd have one of his assistants send them off.

There was nothing I could do to save Thorn and me.

But perhaps I could still save Diesel.

HIS ASSISTANT MADE ME WAIT FOR FIFTEEN MINUTES before she ushered me inside.

Vincent Hunt was definitely pissed. His eyebrows were furrowed, and his dark eyes looked black like drops of oil. He was seething in silence, his jaw clenched just the way Diesel's did when he was ticked about something. Their striking resemblance allowed me to read him well even when he was just a stranger.

"Good morning." I lowered myself into the chair facing his desk.

He didn't have a greeting in return. His hands were together on his knee, and he stared at me like I wasn't welcome in his presence. He always gave me respect even if he didn't like what I had to say. But now that respect was gone.

"You've heard about Thorn and me."

"Bits here and there."

"Diesel and I have decided we want to be together—even if you do leak those photos."

"Good to know. Now if you'll excuse me, I have a story to share with the world."

It still shocked me how spiteful he was. He was so angry with his son that he couldn't see straight. His hurt and love had blended together so well that he misinterpreted it for rage. He didn't know how to digest his misery, so he sabotaged Diesel in every way he could—even though it wouldn't make him feel better. "Thorn and I were really good friends." Speaking in past tense still got me choked up, but I refused to show emotion in front of Vincent. "Our engagement was a business arrangement. When I fell in love with your son, it complicated things. I ended my relationship with Thorn because I knew I couldn't live without your son. You can ruin my reputation all you want, but it's not going to change anything. I intend to spend the rest of my life with Diesel—for better or worse."

He hadn't moved an inch, his hostile gaze still burning holes into my skin.

"So, I'm going to be your daughter-in-law someday."

"First, I'd have to have him as a son—which I don't."

I was grateful Diesel would never hear that comment. I'd take it to the grave. "I know you love Diesel. You can backpedal all you want, but I already know the truth."

Aggressive silence.

"You have a chance to take a step forward in the right direction."

"I have nothing to say to that arrogant asshole."

"You don't have to say anything at all," I said gently. "But you can do something that will mean a great deal to him."

Vincent Hunt watched me with the same dark expression Diesel sometimes gave. It was guarded but absorbing at the same time.

"Diesel would do anything for me. So, if you hurt me, it hurts him more. If you release those photos, people aren't going to care about him as much as me. People will question my integrity and my credibility. Women see me as a role model, and soon the people who once looked up to me will call me a whore. They're getting a version of the story that's inaccurate. You're sending my reputation to the grave, making me serve a sentence for a crime I didn't commit. If you publish those photos, Diesel will never forgive you for it. He'll hate you for the rest of his life. But if you don't publish them...it'll mean something to him. It'll change the way he thinks of you. It'll give you a chance to make things right between you...eventually."

Vincent Hunt shifted his gaze away, thinking about my words without letting me see his reaction. He kept his hands on his knee, his fingers shifting slightly in their hold.

"Take the first step, Vincent. Call him and tell him you won't publish those photos."

He rubbed his jaw, his thick stubble grown into a full beard.

"It won't happen overnight, but your relationship will start to change. You'll leave the door open for reconciliation."

"You're forgetting that I already crossed a line by obtaining the photos to begin with. I purposely went out of my way to blackmail my own son. I've taken a company away from him, and I threatened to ruin your life if he didn't cooperate. Why the hell would you want Diesel and me to work things out? You should despise me, Titan. Any self-respecting person would." He looked away, staring at the other window inside his office. His jaw tensed and relaxed as he rubbed his fingers across his chin. He hid his vulnerability the same way Diesel did, bottling it up inside.

"I don't despise you, Vincent."

He shifted his gaze back to me.

"I can't justify your actions, but I can understand them. You love your son, and you're hurt that he turned his back on you. He hurt your pride and broke your heart at the exact same time. You don't know to handle that, and your wife isn't here to help you. You're lost. I see it when I look at you."

His voice erupted as a whisper. "You don't know me, Titan."

"Then correct me if I'm wrong."

He only gave me his silence.

"I know it's complicated. If it weren't, I could sit the two of you down and have you talk it out. But this is going to be difficult. You need to start somewhere, and I think this is where it should begin. Don't publish those photos."

He stared at me hard.

"Diesel is just as angry as you are. I can barely get him to talk about you without him storming off. He has a lot of issues he needs to take care of. But beneath all of that, he just wants you to be his father."

"He said that?"

I couldn't lie to him. "No. But I know that's how he feels."

Vincent put up his guard again.

"Which means you also need to make things right with Brett. Not right this second…but eventually."

"He's a grown man and doesn't need me. I doubt he wants anything to do with me."

"You'd be surprised. Every person needs their parent —no matter how old they get."

"You never explained why you're doing this," he said quietly. "You're going out of your way to reunite me with my son, but I don't see what you get out of it."

"I don't get anything out of it," I said honestly. "But I love Diesel, and I want him to have his father in his life. My father has been dead for ten years. Not a day goes by that I don't miss him. The both of you are still alive and healthy. Every minute you're angry with each other is a wasted opportunity. I don't want Diesel to wait until the last minute and live in regret. I don't want both of you to wait until it's too late."

If Vincent took my words to heart, he hid it. He kept up the same stone face as he did before. He blocked me out just the way his son did when he was angry. He wouldn't let me cross a line, and I suspected he wouldn't allow anyone to. "You remind me of my late wife."

That was the last thing I'd expected him to say.

"And Diesel reminds me of myself. I loved her the

way he loves you. I saw the way he looked at you from across the room...and it reminded me of the way I looked at her as she walked down the aisle toward me."

It was a precious thing to say, and he chose to share it with me. He spoke so plainly, but there was a hint of emotion in his eyes. "I apologize for ever for jeopardizing your relationship. That was wrong of me."

An apology from Vincent Hunt. I'd never thought that was possible. "I accept your apology."

He gave me a slight nod. "I'll consider your advice."

I took that as a dismissal. I'd done the most I could under the circumstances. I had chipped away at his stone wall, but there were still feet of concrete to get through. I had to quit while I was ahead. "Goodbye, Mr. Hunt." I walked to the door.

"Titan."

I turned around and faced him, unsure what he might say now.

"My son is a lucky man."

15

HUNT

I HAD a plan to reunite Titan and Thorn, but I knew Titan wouldn't go for it.

She'd be pissed, actually.

But I wanted her to be happy, to have both of us in her life. Tragedy was the only thing that brought people together, and that was the only thing that would make Thorn forget his anger and come running.

I was still thinking it over when Natalie spoke through my intercom. "Mr. Vincent Hunt is on the line." She didn't shake in fear this time. That was a good sign.

"I told you not to take his calls anymore." I wanted nothing to do with my father. The only reason he was calling now was to threaten me with those photos. He knew Titan and I beat him to the punch by breaking up her relationship with Thorn. He wasn't happy that I outsmarted him—again.

"He was insistent."

"I don't care."

"And he said he would just come down here if I didn't patch him through..."

A phone call was definitely preferable to a personal visit. "I'll take it."

"Line one."

I grabbed the phone and slammed my finger onto the button. "What?" I wasn't going to be tactful anymore. I was just going to be rude and loud. My father had bullied me for too long, and I wasn't putting up with it anymore. Titan and I were together, and now he had nothing to manipulate me with anymore. "What the fuck do you want?"

My father didn't rise to my anger. "Having a bad day?"

My eyebrows arched at his cool attitude. "It was great until you called."

"I'm sorry I dampened your afternoon. I'll make it quick."

"Please do."

"I won't release those photos of you and Titan."

I heard what he said, but I waited for more. There was always something more when it came to him, some kind of catch. "If I do what?"

"You don't need to do anything, Diesel. I'm just telling you I won't be using those photos against you."

Now my suspicions were higher. "Why?"

My father paused for a long time. "I don't want to."

"I don't understand." All my father cared about was sabotaging me. Now he didn't want to?

"I've destroyed them. I had them on a hard drive, which I just mailed to you. The physical copies have been shredded. Just thought it would give you peace of mind."

Ordinarily, it would. But when it came to my psychotic father, it just put me on edge. "It doesn't give me peace of mind. You expect me to believe you're calling a truce when all you've done is sabotage my life?"

My father was silent.

"Sorry if I'm a little hesitant."

He was still quiet.

So I turned quiet.

"Make of it what you will. I won't be using those photos against you. That's all I wanted to say."

"You—"

Click.

———————

When I went home after work, I packed an entire suitcase of clothes. I hung up my suits carefully, packed my workout clothes, and brought along everything else I needed. By the time, I walked out of there, I had two different suitcases stuffed with my things.

I wasn't leaving Titan anytime soon.

My driver dropped me off, and I rode the elevator to the top floor. I wouldn't have to ask for a key because she didn't have a front door. The doors slid apart, and I stepped into her penthouse, smelling the mixture of flowers, perfume, and power. "Baby?" I stripped off my jacket and hung it on the coatrack.

She emerged out of the kitchen, barefoot because she kicked off her heels the second she was out of the public eye. Her eyes glowed like it was Christmas morning, and her smile was even more touching.

It was exactly what I wanted.

She ran across the floor and jumped right into my arms.

I caught her and held her against me, my smile matching hers. Her hair tickled my neck, and her perfume overcame my senses. She was lighter than a pillow, and soft just like one too. My arms locked around her waist, and I held her feet above the ground, staring at the woman who'd claimed my heart the second I laid eyes on her. "I missed you too."

"What were you doing in the kitchen?"

"Making dinner."

"For two?" I asked hopefully.

"Yes."

I was loving this already. "I hope it doesn't burn." I carried her into the bedroom down the hall, leaving my suitcases behind as I headed straight for the bed. I dropped her on top, unzipped her pencil skirt, and peeled away her layers until she was naked underneath me.

Perky tits.

Tiny waist.

Womanly hips.

And a perfect pussy.

My clothes were gone an instant later, and I climbed on top of her. The rest of the world melted away as I looked down into her beautiful face. Her legs were already spread, and her thighs hugged my hips. Her hands moved up my chest and around my neck, the desire heavy in her eyes.

It felt like our first time, the beginning of a lifetime of lovemaking. I wasn't ashamed to admit I wanted her for the rest of my life. I didn't care if she thought it was too soon or too fast.

She was the one.

I fucking knew it.

My dick slid into her soaked pussy immediately, and I was greeted by the tightness I'd become used to. There was no other pussy on the planet like this. I'd had many, and none of them compared to hers. No other woman compared to Titan, the strongest and proudest woman I'd ever known. She would give birth to my sons, who would grow to be real men. She would give me daughters who would be just as smart and strong. She would give me everything that money couldn't buy.

"Oh god..." She pulled me harder into her, her nipples sharpening like the edge of a knife. Her mouth was open, revealing her small teeth and sexy tongue. The second I was inside her, she was a mess underneath me. She whimpered and moaned, her nails digging into my skin. She breathed hard before she bit her bottom lip. "I'm already going to come..." Her hands dragged down my strong chest, her pussy tightening around me.

I pushed her harder into the bed, making her sink into the mattress as she took my enormous cock. I was a little harder than usual, aroused after my long dry spell. And I was harder because I finally had the woman I wanted.

She believed me.

That was the biggest turn-on of all.

Her hands moved to my ass, and she tugged me into her as her head rolled back. "Yes..."

I pounded into her harder, driving her into an orgasm that was full of screams.

"Diesel..." Her eyes opened, and she looked right into my face, her cheeks red and her eyes on fire. Her tits shook up and down from my thrusts, making her look like my ultimate fantasy. Her pussy clenched around me, and the stars reflected in her eyes. She whimpered like she was crying, tears of pleasure streaking from the corners of her eyes. She gripped my lower back and released another moan as her climax intensified.

I loved watching her come.

When she finished, she kissed me hard on the mouth and ran her fingers through my hair. She clung to me harder as if that orgasm wasn't enough for her. Now she wanted me more, wanted me deeper and harder. "Give it to me, Diesel. I want it."

Instinctively, I gripped the back of her neck and released a carnal groan. If she wanted me to last a long time, she should have held back those words a little longer. Nothing I enjoyed more than pumping my woman full of come. "Wider."

She opened her legs for me, pinning them back until her knees touched her rib cage.

I pushed myself in there deeper, harder. Her slickness increased with her orgasm, and I felt my lungs shake because it felt so incredible. I wanted to give it to her as forceful and good as I possibly could. There was going to be a lot, mounds of it.

"Please..." She wrapped her arms around my shoulders and tugged me into her body, bringing us as close together as possible. She moaned every time I thrust inside her, and her legs shook as she waited for me to release.

When I came, it was so damn good. A colossal orgasm that could bring me to my knees. I released inside her perfect pussy and gave her everything I had. I stuffed her completely full, forcing some of my come to push around my cock and out of her entrance. She was too small, my dick was too big, and I gave too much. "Baby…" Sex had never been so great with anyone else. She wasn't just amazing in the sack. I adored this woman with everything that I had. I worshiped the ground she walked on, cherished her with endless kisses of devotion. She'd taken every piece of me, keeping my heart and soul for her to enjoy. She would have them forever, as long as I lived and even after I died.

Even if she left me, she would still have them.

Because I could never give them to someone else.

WE SHOWERED, HAD DINNER, AND THEN GOT READY for bed.

I was used to being kicked out once the fun was over. She dismissed me with just a look, silently telling me I shouldn't even try to sleep over. We used to sleep beside each other almost every night, but once the shit hit the fan, I was only welcome in her bed for one reason.

But now all of that had changed.

I unpacked my suitcases and hung up my clothes in the closet. She made room for me in one of her drawers, so I placed my dress socks and boxers inside. The nightstand on my side of the bed was emptied, so I could put whatever I wanted inside.

She shared her space with me.

I lay beside her in bed and listened to her gentle breathing. I'd missed that sound, the beautiful melody that helped me drift to sleep. She cleared my thoughts with her presence, bringing me a swell of peace I couldn't find anywhere else.

She turned on her side and faced me, dressed in one of my black t-shirts. Her makeup was gone, but she was still the most gorgeous woman in Manhattan. I loved her fair skin, her perfect complexion. I loved the way her green eyes remained bright even without mascara. I loved that her inner beauty was visible to me at all times.

I held her close to me, taking the position we always took when we were in bed together. Her leg was hiked over my hip, long and smooth. My hand rested on her ass, the beautiful flesh I always wanted to sink my teeth into. Her arm was hooked around my neck, her face just inches from mine.

My father kept his word and didn't leak those pictures to the world. Our relationship remained a secret, and we enjoyed every second of our privacy. I didn't know what to make of my father's abrupt change in behavior, but I thought I should share it with her. "My father called me today."

Instead of looking surprised or concerned, her expression didn't change—at all.

"He said he wouldn't leak our photos to the press—but he didn't say why."

Her hand slid down my bare chest, feeling the muscles underneath her fingertips. "That was nice of him."

"Nice?" I raised an eyebrow. "I don't know about that."

"He didn't ask for anything in return, right?"

"No. He even sent his drive of the photos to my office."

She continued to rub my chest. "Maybe he realized he was wrong. Maybe he's trying to make amends with you."

My father had ignored me for the past ten years. We'd stand in the same room together, and he would pretend I didn't exist. How could a father ever treat his son that way? I didn't go out of my way to heal the relationship either, but I wasn't the one who did something wrong. "Unlikely."

"Then what other explanation is there?"

My eyes shifted back and forth as I looked into her gaze. A conclusion didn't come to mind. "My father is a psychopath. I won't pretend to understand the way he thinks."

"Well, I think he's trying to take a step in the right direction."

"Why?"

Her hand slid down to my stomach, her fingers tracing the grooves of the muscles in my abdomen. Her eyes turned down as she watched her movements.

She never looked away—unless she had something to hide. "Baby?"

After a sigh, she shifted her gaze back to me. "I stopped by your father's office yesterday."

Alarms went off in my head, feeling betrayal. Titan went behind my back and spoke to my father. My nostrils flared in rage, but then I quickly pulled myself back to a state of calm. She was free to do whatever she wanted. She'd become part of this feud because she'd been the recipient of his revenge too. And whatever actions she took, I knew she would keep my best interests at heart. "And what was said?"

"I asked him not to release those photos."

"And he listened to you?" I shouldn't be surprised that Titan could accomplish something I never could. My father was more stubborn than a bull. And when he came head-to-head with another bull, it was worse.

"Yes."

My father had no problem destroying my life, but if

Titan made a request, he didn't mind accommodating it. I was his son, and she was just a stranger. It was wrong on so many levels.

"I told him you would never forgive him if he released those photos."

My eyes focused on her face, numb to her fingertips as she touched me.

"He's angry with you over a few things. He knows you're angry with him. But he wants to reconcile with you...eventually. He doesn't want to take a relationship off the table altogether. So I told him to take the first step toward making things right. That's why he sent you those photos, as an act of truce."

As much as I wanted to deny it, her words meant something to me. My father was tense and quiet over the phone, but he wasn't hostile. He did exactly what he said he would. He halted his fire and didn't destroy Titan. She was right when she said I would never forgive him for hurting her. He'd obviously listened.

"What are you thinking?"

"A million things."

"Care to share?" Her hand moved up my back and into my hair, where she gently massaged the strands. Her fingertips were heavy with love, and she touched me in a special way. It was sexy but affectionate at the same time.

"I hate him. But at the same time, I appreciate what he did."

"I told you he loved you."

"I think you're getting carried away."

"I don't." She held my gaze with strong green eyes. "He took the first step, Diesel. Now you should take the next one."

"You're forgetting all the shit he did before this. He does one right thing, and he's vindicated?"

"I didn't say that."

"You're acting like it. That man is evil."

"No, he's not," she said gently. "He's your father."

"I haven't had a father in ten years." I'd never forget the way he treated Brett, always neglecting him and giving Jax and me all the attention. "And now I'm a grown-ass man who doesn't need one."

"Every child needs a parent."

"Not me."

"Diesel." Her hand moved to my cheek, where she rested her fingertips. "I'm going to say something to you, and you'd better listen to me." Her green eyes were bright despite the darkness. She possessed so much beauty without even trying. She was gorgeous from head to toe, inside and out.

"I always listen to you, baby."

"You're going to listen to me even more now," she whispered. "My father wasn't a perfect man."

The second she mentioned her late father, I tensed.

"Money was always a problem. When he was in

between jobs, he drank a lot. Sometimes he wouldn't come home at all. He got down on his luck and sank into his depression. When he crawled out and got another job, he was better. But it was a vicious cycle with him. Every time he apologized, he meant it. I always forgave him, even though I knew he would relapse over and over. He was far from perfect—but he was still my father. I loved him as much as he loved me. We always stood beside each other no matter what. I wish he could see me now, see what I've become. I wish he were still alive so I could take care of him, show him he would never have to worry about money ever again. I wish I could make up for all those difficult years we had." Despite the painful topic, she spoke with strength. Her voice didn't shake even as the emotion grew in her eyes. "My father is gone, and I'll never see him again. But your father is still here, Diesel. He's had his rough years. He was never the same after your mother passed away. He never expected to be a single father. He may be rich, but he's suffered. Like my father, he's not perfect. He's made his share of mistakes. But he's still here—and he loves you."

ALSO BY VICTORIA QUINN

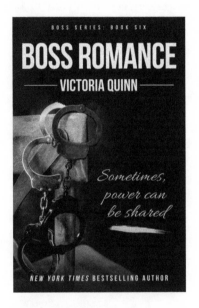

Order Now

CPSIA information can be obtained
at www.ICGtesting.com
Printed in the USA
LVHW02s0044280818
588281LV00001B/203/P